符号中国 SIGNS OF CHINA

唐 诗

THE POETRY OF TANG DYNASTY

"符号中国"编写组 ◎ 编著

中央民族大学出版社
China Minzu University Press

图书在版编目(CIP)数据

唐诗：汉文、英文 /"符号中国"编写组编著. —北京：中央民族大学出版社，2024.3
（符号中国）
ISBN 978-7-5660-2318-6

Ⅰ.①唐⋯ Ⅱ.①符⋯ Ⅲ.①唐诗－诗歌欣赏－汉、英 Ⅳ.①I207.227.42

中国国家版本馆CIP数据核字（2024）第017714号

符号中国：唐诗 THE POETRY OF TANG DYNASTY

编　　著	"符号中国"编写组
策划编辑	沙　平
责任编辑	满福玺
英文指导	李瑞清
英文编辑	邱　械
美术编辑	曹　娜　郑亚超　洪　涛
出版发行	中央民族大学出版社
	北京市海淀区中关村南大街27号　邮编：100081
	电话：（010）68472815（发行部）　传真：（010）68933757（发行部）
	（010）68932218（总编室）　　　　（010）68932447（办公室）
经 销 者	全国各地新华书店
印 刷 厂	北京兴星伟业印刷有限公司
开　　本	787 mm×1092 mm　1/16　印张：11.125
字　　数	144千字
版　　次	2024年3月第1版　2024年3月第1次印刷
书　　号	ISBN 978-7-5660-2318-6
定　　价	58.00元

版权所有　侵权必究

"符号中国"丛书编委会

唐兰东　巴哈提　杨国华　孟靖朝　赵秀琴

本册编写者

李葳葳

前言 Preface

唐诗在中国几乎无人不知，无人不晓，连三岁孩童也能吟出一两首。唐诗里有中国五千年历史中繁盛的王朝——唐朝的缩影，有才华横溢的诗人们的喜怒哀乐。唐诗中既有华美精致的辞藻，也有和谐优美的韵律；既

The poetry of Tang Dynasty (618-907) is well-known in China; even a three-year-old child can recite one or two poems, in which we can see the epitome of the most flourishing dynasty, Tang Dynasty and the various emotions of these talented poets. It is a form of art combined with gorgeous rhetoric and harmonious rhythm, which is both of romance and reality. The Tang poetry is a treasure left by the Tang Dynasty and also the mainstay of Chinese classic culture, as well as the symbol of elegance and gracefulness. For anyone who wants to feel the charm of language, the poetry of Tang Dynasty cannot be missed.

有浪漫，也有现实。唐诗是唐朝人留给中国和世界的绝代珍品。唐诗是中国古典文化的中流砥柱，也是高贵典雅的象征。读者朋友们想要领略语言文化的魅力，唐诗不应该错过。

此书旨在呈现唐朝的著名诗人和唐诗作品以及唐诗的相关知识，希望读者可以从中体会到唐诗的韵味，欣赏唐诗的美妙，增加对唐诗的了解。学习和吟咏唐诗，可以提高自身的修养和品位，增强文化底蕴，也是了解中国文化的必经之路。

This book is to introduce the famous poets of that time, their epochal works, and the relevant knowledge. Hope that the readers can learn the charm of Tang poetry, appreciate its beauty and have a deeper understanding about this special literary form. Learning and reciting Tang poetry can raise one's own accomplishment and taste and enhance cultural heritage, which is also an inevitable path to get to know the Chinese culture.

目 录 Contents

璀璨唐诗
Splendid Tang Poetry 001

大唐盛世
The Golden Age of the Great Tang Dynasty 002

诗歌巅峰
Peak of Poetry 009

群星闪耀
Brilliant Poets 014

唐诗分期
Stages of Tang Poetry 017

唐诗魅力
Glamour of Tang Poetry 025

唐诗知识
Knowledge of Tang Poetry 031

唐诗的体裁
Genres of Tang Poetry 032

唐诗的题材
Themes of Tang Poetry 042

唐诗的诗派
Schools of Tang Poetry 062

1

著名诗人与唐诗作品
Famous Poets and Works 073

"诗仙"李白
"Poetry Immortal" Li Bai 074

"诗圣"杜甫
"Poetry Sage" Du Fu 084

"诗魔"白居易
"Poetry Wizard" Bai Juyi 091

王维
Wang Wei 100

李贺
Li He 105

孟浩然
Meng Haoran 111

王昌龄
Wang Changling 116

杜牧
Du Mu 121

李商隐
Li Shangyin 127

唐朝女诗人
Poetesses of Tang Dynasty 133

脍炙人口的唐诗
Celebrated Tang Poetries 147

璀璨唐诗
Splendid Tang Poetry

　　唐诗，因唐朝的强大繁荣而生，也随着唐王朝的命运变化而起起伏伏。唐诗是唐朝的写照，也因为唐朝而奠定了其在中国文坛辉煌耀眼的地位，因此本部分主要介绍唐朝及唐诗的历史背景。

Tang poetry was born at the historic moment when the Tang Dynasty(618-907) reached its formidable and prosperous age and fluctuated with its fickle fate. Tang poetry is the reflection of the Tang Dynasty owing to which it has a spectacular position in Chinese literary arena. So this chapter is mainly about the Tang Dynasty and the historical background of Tang Poetry.

> **大唐盛世**

在中国两千多年的封建王朝历史中,唐朝(618—907)是当之无愧的黄金时代,也是当时与阿拉伯帝国齐名的世界强国。公元755年前的唐朝,无论是政治、经济、文化还是对外交往,都发展到了顶峰——经济贸易空前繁荣,政治管理科学开明,精神文化丰富多样,对外交流频繁广泛。人民的生活物质富足,社会环境稳定祥和,甚至出现了"夜不闭户、路不拾遗"的和谐景象。妇女在唐朝的社会地位得到了很大的提升,甚至有机会像男人一样参与社会生活,唐朝也是中国唯一出现女皇帝(武则天)的封建王朝。各民族文化得到同等尊重和充分融合,人们的精神世界也

> **The Golden Age of the Great Tang Dynasty**

During the more than two thousand years when feudal dynasties ruled the China, the Tang Dynasty fully deserves the title of "Golden Age", which was also the mighty country eponymous to the Arab Empire. Before 755 A.D., no matter on the politics, economy, culture or the foreign affairs, the Tang Dynasty had reached its peak of flourishing trade, scientific and liberal political management, diversified spiritual culture, and frequent and wide external communication. People were living plentiful lives in a harmonious society, even having the pictures of "Doors are unbolted at night, and no one picks up and pockets anything lost on the road". The status of women was raised greatly and they even could have the same

● 唐高祖李渊像

李渊，字叔德，原是隋朝贵族，隋末天下大乱时，李渊乘势从太原起兵，攻占长安。公元618年，李渊称帝，改国号"唐"，定都长安（今陕西西安），为唐高祖。

Portrait of Emperor Li Yuan of the Tang Dynasty

Li Yuan, with a courtesy name of Shude, originally was an aristocrat of the Sui Dynasty (581-618). During the turbulence of the late Sui Dynasty, Li Yuan seized the opportunity and revolted from Taiyuan, and finally occupied Chang'an. In 618 A.D., he proclaimed himself as the new emperor, became the first Emperor of the Tang Dynasty, and changed the dynasty title as *Tang*, and determined Chang'an (present Xi'an City, Shaanxi Province) as its capital city.

得到了最大的丰富。百姓在安居乐业的同时，纷纷写诗、郊游，以及组织参加各种各样的宴会等娱乐活动。

唐朝凭着强盛国力雄踞东方，周边的邻国纷纷来唐朝朝贺进贡、学习唐朝先进的技术和文化，促进

opportunities as men did. And that's when the only female emperor, Empress Wu Zetian, ascended the throne. Cultures of various ethnic groups were equally respected and fully fused together. The mental world of people was enriched largely. Living and working in peace and contentment, they also wrote poems, went on an outing and organized many kinds of feasts and recreational activities.

With its powerful national strength, the Tang Dynasty imposingly stood at the east, and the neighboring countries constantly visited and paid tribute to it, at the same time, to learn its advanced techniques and culture, which actually promoted the communication between the Tang Dynasty and the external cultures. Up to now, there are more or less cultural characteristics and historical relics of the Tang Dynasty preserved in many countries' cultures from which the important position and profound influence of China at that time can be reflected.

The capital city of the Tang Dynasty, Chang'an and its accompanying capital city Luoyang were the world-famous international metropolis, where the stores were full of various exotic goods and were strolling among the streets and

003

璀璨唐诗 Splendid Tang Poetry

了唐朝与外来文化的交流。至今，在许多国家的文化中都或多或少地保留了唐朝时的文化特点和历史遗迹，从中可以看出中国唐朝在当时世界上的重要地位和深远影响力。

　　唐朝的首都长安、陪都洛阳是当时举世闻名的国际大都市，坊间各国的商品琳琅满目，身着各种奇装异服的外国人穿梭于大街小巷之中。唐王朝以海纳百川的胸怀和气魄，施行开明的对外政策，吸引大批波斯和阿拉伯商人通过世界闻名

small alleys. With generous mind, the court applied moderate foreign policies and attracted bunches of Persian and Arabian merchants through the famous Silk Road coming to Chang'an, Luoyang, Guangzhou, Quanzhou and other coastal cities to settle down. While keeping a friendly contact with the neighboring countries, the court also maintained a powerful military force to insure the safety of the Silk Road and the border areas. And it once extended the influence to the Aral Sea of the Central Asia

● **唐太宗李世民像**

唐太宗李世民是李渊之子，唐朝的第二位皇帝。他即位为帝后，积极听取群臣的意见，努力学习文治天下，使社会出现了国泰民安的局面，开创了历史上的"贞观之治"，是史上最出名的政治家与明君之一。

Portrait of Emperor Li Shimin of the Tang Dynasty

Emperor Li Shimin of the Tang Dynasty was the son of Li Yuan and the second emperor of the Tang Dynasty. After ascending the throne, he took officials' advices actively and studied hard to manage state affairs by civilized manners. Therefore, Li Shimin created the prosperous and harmonious situation and initiated the Zhenguan Times (Zhenguan is the period title of Li Shimin's reign), who is a famous politician and wise emperor in history.

的"丝绸之路"来到长安、洛阳等地及广州、泉州等沿海城市定居。在与周边各国友好往来的同时,唐王朝以庞大的军事力量维护着丝绸之路及边境地区的安全,其势力范围一度到达中亚的咸海,北到今西伯利亚,南到今泰国境内。唐王朝以巨大的军费开支为代价,常年派重兵驻守边境以示国力强大。

westward and today's Siberia northward, today's Thailand southward. The Tang Dynasty cost huge military expenditure to send massive forces to guard the frontier and show its formidable power.

The An-Shi Rebellion (755-763) became the crucial historic event which led to the decline of the Tang Dynasty. The court set the main troops at the frontier, which resulted in the weakness of

- 《步辇图》阎立本(唐)

《步辇图》取材于唐贞观十五年(641)吐蕃首领松赞干布与文成公主联姻的事件,描绘了唐太宗李世民接见吐蕃使臣禄东赞的情景。吐蕃是公元7—9世纪古代藏族建立的政权,在松赞干布统治时期达到鼎盛。唐与吐蕃交流十分密切,汉文化的输入对吐蕃社会起了巨大的促进作用,吐蕃文化对汉族也有一定的影响。

Painting of Imperial Parade, by Yan Liben, Tang Dynasty (618-907)

Painting of Imperial Parade was created based on the allied marriage of Sontzen Gampo the ruler of the Tubo Kingdom and Chinese princess Wencheng in the 15th year of Period Zhenguan (641), depicting the scene when Emperor Li Shimin received the Tubo envoy, Lu Dongzan. Tubo was an authority set up in 7th-9th century by ancient Tubo people which reached its great prosperity during the reign of Sontzen Gampo. The communication between the Tang Dynasty and Tubo was very intimate. The introduction of Chinese culture made a great promotion to the development of Tubo society, and vice versa.

• 胡人牵骆驼俑（唐）
Clay Statue of an Ethnic Man Leading a Camel (Tang Dynasty, 618-907)

公元755年到763年的"安史之乱"是导致唐王朝由盛转衰的重要历史事件。因将重要兵力放在边境，导致国内防御空虚，安禄山、史思明率领的叛军迅速攻破首都长安。虽然在朝廷君臣力挽狂澜之后，唐王朝得以延续，但国力明显开始衰退，进入了低谷期。不过，作为封建时代的巅峰王朝，唐朝的根基深厚，经济依然很快得到了复苏。

自唐以后，统治者对人民的思想统治越来越严厉，文化的发展也

the domestic defense. An Lushan and Shi Siming led the rebel army and quickly occupied the capital city Chang'an. Although the emperor and the officials turned the situation and prolonged Tang's reign, its national power started to deteriorate distinctly and finally entered the low ebb. But, as the height of the feudal dynasty, it had deep foundation and the economy revived soon.

Ever since the Tang Dynasty, the rulers controlled people's thoughts more and more severely and the development of the culture was also restricted by more and more objective conditions. After that, the representative literatures of each dynasty such as *Ci* of the Song Dynasty, *Qu* of the Yuan Dynasty, and the novels of the Ming and Qing dynasties, were not equivalent to the "Blooming Tang Grandeur" with various kinds, sturdy

- 《杨贵妃上马图》钱选（元）
  Painting of Imperial Concubine Yang Getting on a Horse, by Qian Xuan (Yuan Dynasty, 1206-1368)

受到了越来越多的制约。此后各个朝代的代表文学如宋朝的词、元朝的曲、明清的小说等都不同于唐诗"百花齐放、笔力雄壮"，蕴含于

style and imposing manner created by Tang poetry, and the positive and heroic spiritual state contained in the poetry was also no longer in existence. So as one of

诗中的那种积极向上、豪迈壮阔的精神状态也不复存在。唐诗作为中国文化的代表之一当之无愧。唐诗是强盛的大唐王朝为中国乃至世界文化做出的重要贡献，至今仍在世界文学之林中傲然屹立。

the representatives of Chinese culture, Tang poetry fully deserves its title. It is a significant contribution to China as well as the world made by the powerful Tang Dynasty, which is still having a vital place among the world literatures.

安史之乱

"安史之乱"是中国历史上一次重要的事件，是唐朝由盛而衰的转折点。"安"指安禄山和其子安庆绪，"史"指史思明和其子史朝义，"安史之乱"是指他们起兵反对唐王朝的一次叛乱。"安史之乱"自唐玄宗天宝十四年（755）至唐代宗广德元年（763）结束，前后达七年之久。这次历史事件，是当时社会各种矛盾所促成的，对唐朝后期的影响巨大。

An-Shi Rebellion (755-763)

An-Shi Rebellion (755-763), is an important historic event and also the turning point of the Tang Dynasty, from blooming to decline. "An" indicates the rebel forces' leader An Lushan and his son An Qingxu, and "Shi" indicates the leader Shi Siming and his son Shi Chaoyi. It was an insurrection against the Tang Dynasty which was initiated by them, lasting as long as seven years, from the 14th year of Period Tianbao (755) of the reign of Emperor Li Longji to the 1st year of Period Guangde (763) of the reign of Emperor Li Yu. This historic event was catalyzed by various social conflicts of that time and left a huge affection over the late Tang Dynasty.

> 诗歌巅峰

唐朝是中国诗歌史上的鼎盛时期。国家的强大富足和政治开明、以诗取士的选拔制度，以及文人对诗歌创作技巧的不懈探索，造就了唐诗的辉煌成就，使之成为中国文化宝库里永不褪色的瑰宝。在经历其后漫长的一千多年的沧桑巨变之后，保存至今的唐诗数量仍有近五万首。唐代书籍主要靠纸质手抄流传，在十个多世纪之后还能有如此多的作品传世，可见其长久不衰的艺术魅力和在后代人心目中的崇高地位。

唐朝时，无论是皇帝大臣，还是商人小贩，不管是文人武将，还是妇女儿童，甚至是和尚道士、奴婢等，都会创作吟咏诗歌。唐诗的创作人群不仅广泛，而且成绩斐

> Peak of Poetry

The Tang Dynasty was the heyday in the history of chinese poetry. The mighty and prosperous country, the liberal politics, the official selection system upon writing poems, and the constant exploration of the writing skills accomplished the glorious achievement of Tang poetry and made it an everlasting treasure in Chinese literature. After the great changes in more than one thousand years, there are nearly fifty thousand poems preserved until now. The books of the Tang Dynasty were mainly passed down by paper scripts. After more than ten centuries, there are still so many works widely recognized, which demonstrates its permanent artistic charm and the high position in people's mind.

In the Tang Dynasty, emperors and officials, merchants and vendors, scholars

• 彩色釉陶骆驼载乐伎俑（唐）
Color-glazed Clay Statue of Camel Carrying a Musician (Tang Dynasty, 618-907)

然，著名的《全唐诗》作者达2200多人，这在之前的朝代里都是不多见的。

唐诗不仅数量和创作者众多，而且诗歌题材丰富多彩，社会与自然现象的各个方面都成为唐诗吟咏的对象。中国现代著名作家闻一多在评价唐诗的题材时说："凡生活中用到文字的地方，他们一律用诗的形式来写，达到任何事物无不可以入诗的程度。"这也是唐诗读者众多、获得社会各个阶层共鸣的原因之一。

唐诗之所以如此受欢迎，在

and warriors, women and children, even the monks, Taoist priests, prostitutes and servants, they all could write poems. The writers not only were in a wide range, but also made a brilliant achievement. And the famous *Complete Works of Tang Poetry* included more than 2200 poets' works, which was really rare in the former dynasties.

Besides the numerous works and poets, the themes were also full of variety, which included all the aspects of social and natural phenomenons. Famous writer Wen Yiduo once appraised the themes of Tang poetry: "Wherever the character was used, they all wrote in the form of poetry, which reached a realm to be able to express everything with poem." And this is also one of the reasons why the Tang poetry had many readers and well accepted by all the social stratums.

The reason why Tang poetry was so welcomed is its completed genres which possess both the variety and beauty of

于它的体裁完备,既具有音律美,又富有变化。乐府、古诗(包括四言、五言、七言和杂言)、绝句、律诗等多样化的体裁满足了创作的需要。中国古典诗歌体裁从春秋时的《诗经》起,经历了数个朝代文人们的不断探索发展,到了唐朝恰好臻于成熟。多样的表现形式与丰富的诗歌内容完美结合,催生了大批的优秀作品。杜甫的律诗、李白的古风及白居易的乐府诗,更是堪称臻于至境。

唐诗具有如此强大的生命力和创造力,还在于唐诗是唐朝人入朝为官、获得提拔的重要途径。中

rhythm, including *Yuefu* (It originally indicated a government office in the Han Dynasty for collecting folk songs and ballads. While in the Tang Dynasty, it became the name of a genre of poetry.), ancient poetry (including four-character, five-character, seven-character and blend character), *Jueju* (a poem of four lines), *Lvshi* (a poem of eight lines), etc. The diversification of the genres met the needs of creation. The genres of Chinese ancient poetry had been through a constant exploration and development all the way from the *The Book of Songs* of the Spring and Autumn Period (770 B.C.-476 B.C.) to the maturity of the Tang Dynasty. The various expression forms

• **唐代科考场景图**

科举制度是中国古代通过考试选拔官吏的一种制度,源于隋代,兴盛于唐代。唐代的科举考试趋向于以诗赋为主,促进了世人对诗的学习和钻研。唐代大多数诗人都走过科举之路,唐诗百花纷呈的繁荣局面与以诗取士制度密不可分。

Scene of the Imperial Examination of the Tang Dynasty

The imperial examination system, originated in the Sui Dynasty (581-618) and thriving in the Tang Dynasty (618-907), was a regime through which the courtyard selected the officials in ancient China. The examination in the Tang Dynasty tended to prefer testing the ability of writing poetry, which promoted people's study and exploration on the poetry. Most of the poets during that time attended the examination. And the flourishing situation was closely related to the setting of the poetry test in the imperial examination.

国古代文人以儒家"修身齐家治国平天下"为理想。各个朝代选拔人才的方式不尽相同，唐朝的特殊之

and rich contents were combined perfectly and spurred the emergence of a great bunch of fascinating works. Du Fu's *Lvshi*, Li Bai's ancient poetries and Bai Juyi's *Yuefu*, all represent the top-class standard.

The great vitality and creative ability of Tang poetry also depended on the fact that writing Tang poetry was an important official selection and promotion approach. Ancient scholars used the motto of Confucian, "Self-cultivation, regulating the family, ruling the state and the world" as their ideal. The methods of selection were different from one and another in each dynasty. And the specialty of the Tang Dynasty was that they used the poetry as the evaluation of officials. As long as whoever was good at writing poetry, he could get the chance to be recommended. So the enthusiasm of poetry writing in the Tang Dynasty upsurged more than any other ages.

- 康熙皇帝御笔亲书的唐诗条幅（清）
  Vertical Scroll of Tang Poetry by Emperor Kangxi (Qing Dynasty, 1616-1911)

处就在于以诗取士，只要诗歌写得好，就有机会获得赏识，所以唐朝文人创作诗歌的热情空前高涨。

唐诗的最大特色在于它内在的灵魂和气魄。唐朝是中国历史上强大的封建帝国，唐诗的整体特征正反映出唐人气壮山河的自信与雄浑豪迈的激情，这种心胸气概在唐诗里就表现为"盛唐气象"。哪怕在经历"安史之乱"走向衰微之后，文人的诗歌创作仍然追慕着这种气象。"盛唐气象"不仅感动了唐朝人自己，也是唐朝送给后人的珍贵礼物。

唐诗的文字中不乏磅礴恢宏的气势，亦不缺少缠绵悱恻的情致。它可以在幽深的意境营造中表达真情，又可以在生活琐事中蕴含哲理。以至于后人不管是想要抒发内心感受抑或写景状物的时候，都不忘引用几句唐诗。

The biggest feature of Tang poetry is its internal soul and spirit. It was born in the most powerful Chinese feudalist empire. Its main character was to reflect the confidence and passion of the people in that age, which was called "Blooming Tang Grandeur" in Tang poetry. Even after the An-Shi Rebellion (755-763) when the empire was on the wane, the poets still pursued this particular spirit which not only moved themselves but also was a precious gift left to their descendants.

There is majestic vigor between the lines of Tang poetry as well as sentimental temperament. It can express the true feelings through profound conception and also reveal the philosophy hidden in daily trivia. So when later generations want to convey their internal feelings or describe the objects and scenes, they will not forget to quote some lines of Tang poetry.

> 群星闪耀

根据现存的资料记载，大约有2200多位姓名可考的唐诗作者来自社会各个阶层。其中不乏帝王后妃，比如唐太宗李世民、唐玄宗李隆基等均有佳作。太宗的作品与他的为人一样干练豁达，颇具豪迈气魄。玄宗本人则是一个多才多艺的帝王，不仅擅长谱曲，爱好文艺、体育，诗歌作品的气势也不输太

> Brilliant Poets

According to the existing documents, there were approximately 2,200 onymous poets from various social stratums, as well as emperors and imperial concubines, like Emperor Li Shimin, and Emperor Li Longji, etc. Works of Emperor Li Shimin was just as generous as his behavior and full of heroic spirit. And Emperor Li Longji himself was multi-talented, not only good at composing but also fond of art and sports. His works could compete with the ones of Emperor Li Shimin. Empress Wu Zetian (624-705) and the most famous Princess Taiping also had works left behind. Besides, almost all the educated

- 玉龙（唐）
Jade Dragon (Tang Dynasty, 618-907)

- **唐玄宗李隆基像**

唐玄宗李隆基，后世又称"唐明皇"，在位初期任用贤臣、整肃吏治，开创了唐朝乃至中国历史上最为鼎盛的时期，史称"开元盛世"。除了在政治上的成就之外，他还是一位多才多艺的皇帝，音乐、舞蹈、书法、诗歌无所不能。

Portrait of Emperor Li Longji of Tang Dynasty
Emperor Li Longji, also called "Emperor Tang Ming" by the later generations, appointed virtuous officials, regulated the government, made great achievements in both political and military spheres and created the greatest prosperity in the Tang Dynasty even in the Chinese history which was called Kaiyuan Flourishing Age. Besides the political success, he was also a multi-talented emperor who was good at music, dancing, calligraphy and poetry.

宗。一代女皇武则天、唐朝第一公主太平公主等皆有作品流传。此外几乎所有受过教育的文人和官员都具备作诗的才能，并创作了大量的作品。上官婉儿创作的诗歌作品甚至丝毫不逊于男人。唐诗辉煌成就的主要贡献者是文人。包括唐诗大家李白、杜甫等在内的许多著名诗人，都曾经出任官职，又因为各种原因而离开官场，他们因在诗坛取得了辉煌的成就而名垂千古。

　　唐诗的作者中还不乏农夫工匠、渔樵胥吏、婢妾等，佚名的佳作也不少。许多有名的诗人曾经从事农耕、渔樵等职业，皎然、寒山则是著名的诗僧。而唐朝三大女诗人中的薛涛就曾经是歌伎，其余两

scholars and officials were capable of writing poetry and wrote a great amount of works. Shangguan Wan'er could write poetry as well as man's works. As the main contributor of the spectacular achievement of Tang poetry, the scholars including Li Bai, Du Fu and other famous poets once took up official posts and then left due to some reasons. They attained a more splendid achievement in poetry writing and had their names engraved in the history.

　　The writers of Tang poetry also included peasants, craftsmen, fishermen, captains, maids as well as some anonymous ones who wrote many masterpieces. Some famous poets were once working in the farmland and fishing along the river. The monk Jiaoran and

位李冶和鱼玄机则是女道士。甚至外国人来到唐朝也会受到熏陶而学会写诗，日本遣唐使阿倍仲麻吕就是其中之一，他不仅能够写出水平很高的唐诗，还跟李白、王维等诗人结下了深厚的友谊。他创作的诗歌《望乡》成为中日文化交流史上具有纪念意义的著名篇章。

Hanshan were famous poets. The Three Poetesses of the Tang Dynasty, Xue Tao was once a singer, and other two, Li Ye and were female Taoist priests. Even foreigners were influenced to learn to write poems. The Japanese envoy Abe no Nakamaro was one of them, who not only could write excellent poems but also made profound friendship with Li Bai, Wang Wei, and other poets. His famous poem *Nostalgia* also became a memorable and distinguished page in the history of cultural communications between Chinese and Japanese.

● 阿倍仲麻吕纪念碑

阿倍仲麻吕纪念碑坐落在陕西省西安市兴庆宫公园，也就是唐代兴庆宫故址，当年阿倍仲麻吕经常出入的地方。碑上镌刻着他的生平业绩以及他的《望乡》和李白的《哭晁卿衡》两首著名诗篇。《望乡》诗写道："翘首望长天，神驰奈良边。三笠山顶上，想又皎月圆。"

Monument of Abe no Nakamaro

The Monument of Abe no Nakamaro was situated in the Xingqing Imperial Palace Park in Xi'an City, Shaanxi Province which was also the original location of the Xingqing Imperial Palace of the Tang Dynasty where he often visited. His lifetime outstanding achievements were engraved on the monument, as well as two famous poems: *Nostalgia* by him and *Crying for Chao Heng* by Li Bai. The *Nostalgia* was said: "Across the fields of heaven casting my gaze, I indulge my thoughts wandering to the Nara City. I wonder whether over the hills of Mikasa, also the bright full moon has risen."

> 唐诗分期

唐诗的发展与唐王朝的命运息息相关，虽然起伏的曲线跟政治上的分期不完全吻合，但大致走向是一致的，所以后世文学史都以初唐、盛唐、中唐和晚唐为唐诗发展的分期。

> Stages of Tang Poetry

The development of the Tang Dynasty was closely related with the fate of the Tang Empire. Though the fluctuating curve didn't exactly fit with the political stages, the rough tendency was the same. So the history of literature of the later generation divided the development of Tang poetry with early Tang, blooming Tang, middle Tang and late Tang.

In the early Tang Dynasty, the leftover was waiting to be rebuilt and the new empire just unveiled its vitality. The poetry of the former dynasties also needed to be improved. This is the early Tang. As time went by, the country

• 鎏金熊纹六曲银盘（唐）
Gilded Six-petal Silver Plate with Gold Bear Pattern (Tang Dynasty, 618-907)

璀璨唐诗 Splendid Tang Poetry

唐朝初建时百废待兴，新王朝的朝气初露，前朝诗歌并不完善，有待发展，此为初唐；随着时光推移，唐朝国力达到鼎盛时期，唐诗也达到了顶峰，出现了百花齐放的繁荣景象，此为盛唐；"安史之乱"对国家经济政治文化造成严重破坏，唐王朝的国力逐渐下滑，进入缓慢衰落的阶段，唐诗也逐步走向成熟，开始出现衰落的态势，此为中唐；到了唐朝末期，唐诗出现了形式多样、绚丽多彩、音韵优美等独具魅力的艺术风格特点，此为晚唐。每个时期的诗风各有千秋，诗人则各放异彩。

初唐时期的代表诗人是"初唐四杰"——王勃、杨炯、卢照邻、骆宾王，还有"诗骨"陈子昂。他们的创作为唐诗后来的发展奠定了良好的开局。王勃的《送杜少府之任蜀州》、杨炯的《紫骝马》、卢照邻的《长安古意》、骆宾王的《咏鹅》、陈子昂的《登幽州台歌》是他们各自的代表作。其中陈子昂《登幽州台歌》中的千古名句"前不见古人，后不见来者"将时间和空间串联在一起，仅以十个字就纵观古今，瞻前并且顾后，将人

reached its most prosperous period when Tang poetry also got to the top. It appeared the diversified flourishing situation. This is the blooming Tang. An-Shi Rebellion caused a severe catastrophe to the nation's economy, politics and culture. The national power gradually went down and slowly entered into the deteriorating stage. And Tang poetry also matured and started to show the declining tendency. This is the middle Tang. In the late Tang Dynasty, Tang poetry appeared with unique and charming artistic characteristics such as diverse forms and beautiful phonology. This is the late Tang. The style was different and varied in each stage. And the poets also put extraordinary splendor respectively.

The representative poets of the early Tang stage were the "Four Distinguished of Early Tang Dynasty", including Wang Bo, Yang Jiong, Lu Zhaolin, and Luo Binwang, as well as the "Poetry Bone", Chen Zi'ang. Their works established a good foundation for the further development of Tang poetry. Their respective master works were: *Seeing Magistrate Du off to Shu* (*Song Du Shaofu Zhi Ren Shuzhou*) by Wang Bo, *A Red Horse* (*Ziliuma*) by Yang Jiong, *Old Song of Chang'an* (*Chang'an Guyi*)

- **卢照邻像**

卢照邻，字升之，幽州范阳（今河北省涿州市）人。唐代"初唐四杰"之一，擅长古文和七言歌行体古诗，对推动七言古诗的发展有贡献。

Portrait of Lu Zhaolin

Lu Zhaolin, with courtesy name of Sheng Zhi, was born in Fanyang, Youzhou (present Zhuozhou City, Hebei Province), one of the "Four Distinguished of Early Tang Dynasty", who was expert in seven-character lyric style ancient poetry and contributed a lot to the development of this poetry genre.

- **青釉褐彩诗文瓷壶（唐）**

Green Glazed Brown-color Porcelain Pot with Poem Inscription (Tang Dynasty, 618-907)

们的视野扩大到了从过去到将来的无限空间，已经初露唐王朝的壮阔气魄，是盛唐之音的前奏。这一时期的宫体诗虽然在内容题材上受到诟病，但宫体诗艺术上的发展完备对后来律诗的成熟功不可没。

盛唐时期的浪漫主义诗人李白（701—762）和现实主义诗人杜

by Lu Zhaolin, *Goose (Yong E)* by Luo Binwang, and *On Climbing Youzhou Tower (Deng Youzhou Tai Ge)* by Chen Zi'ang. And the famous lines of the *On Climbing Youzhou Tower*, "Where are the saints of the past, and those of the future?" combined the time and space together. With only ten characters, the poet saw through the past and the

- 《宫乐图》佚名（唐）

此图描写后宫嫔妃十人，围坐于一张巨型方桌四周，有的在品茗，有的在行酒令，中央四人吹乐助兴，悠闲自得。

Recreation of the Palace, by Anonymity (Tang Dynasty, 618-907)

This painting depicted ten imperial concubines sitting around a huge square table. Some were having some tea; some were playing drinker's wager game; the four in the middle were playing musical instruments to entertain others. The whole atmosphere was very eased.

甫（712—770）即是这一时期最杰出的代表。李白和杜甫不仅是唐诗最高成就的代表，也是中国文化在世界上的重要代表。他们是世界级的中国古代历史文化名人，代表名篇数不胜数。李白的《梦游天姥吟留别》《行路难》《将进酒》等名篇震古烁今；杜甫的"三吏""三别"及《蜀相》《春夜喜雨》等名

present, showing respect to the preceding era and also freeing imagination on the succeeding age. It expanded people's vision to the limitless space of the past and the future, which had already revealed the magnificent spirit of the blooming Tang and was the prelude of the symphony of the flourishing time. Though the palace poetry of this time was scolded by its content and theme, yet its development and perfection on the art directly contributed to the maturity of the *Lvshi* (a poem of eight lines) afterwards.

The blooming Tang period had two most outstanding representatives: the romantic poet, Li Bai (701-762) and the realistic poet, Du Fu (712-770). They not only stood for the highest achievement of the Tang poetry but also the fascinating Chinese culture in the world. They were the world-class cultural celebrities of ancient Chinese history, who had left countless masterpieces to the descendants. The masterpieces like *Tianmu Mountain Ascended in a Dream* (*Mengyou Tianmu Yin Liubie*), *Difficult Journey* (*Xinglu Nan*), *Bringing In the Wine* (*Qiang Jinjiu*) by Li Bai, are still with great reputation; the famous works like "The Sergeant Trilogy" (*Sanli*), "The Parting Trilogy" (*Sanbie*), *Temple of the Premier*

- 银质开元通宝（唐）

开元通宝是唐朝主要流通货币，一般为铜制，金、银制开元通宝仅限皇家赏赐，供高官显贵玩赏，并不投入流通，因此存世量极小。

Silver *Kaiyuan Tongbao* (Tang Dynasty, 618-907)

Kaiyuan Tongbao was the main circulating coin in the Tang Dynasty. Generally it was made of copper. The gold and silver ones were cast as the award granted by the imperial family or the artwork appreciated by dignitaries, which were usually out of the circulation, so the surviving is in small amounts.

- 狩猎纹高足银杯（唐）

Silver Goblet with Hunting Pattern (Tang Dynasty, 618-907)

篇流传千古。此外田园山水诗派的王维（701—761）、孟浩然（689—740）和边塞诗派的高适（约700—765）、王昌龄（？—约756）等人的诗歌也各具特色，各有千秋。王维的《山居秋暝》、孟浩然的《春晓》、王昌龄的《出塞》、高适的《别董大》等均为佳作。盛唐时期，人才辈出，共同营造了雄壮浑厚的"盛唐气象"，并影响了后世几代诗人。

of Shu (*Shuxiang*), *Seasonable Rain in Spring Night* (*Chunye Xiyu*) by Du Fu are passed down through generations. And the poems of the landscape and pastoral poets like Wang Wei (701-761), Meng Haoran (689-740) and the ones of the frontier fortress poets like Gao Shi (approx.700-765), Wang Changling (?-756) are also with respective features and have their own merits, including *Autumn Evening in the Mountains* (*Shanju Qiuming*) by Wang Wei, *Spring Morning* (*Chunxiao*) by Meng Haoran, *On the Frontier* (*Chusai*) by Wang Changling, *A Farewell with Dong Da* (*Bie Dong*

- 《捣练图》张萱（唐）

这幅《捣练图》描绘了贵族妇女捣练缝衣的工作场面，从事同一活动的人由于身份、年龄、分工的不同，动作、表情也各不相同。图画将其描绘得惟妙惟肖，反映出盛唐崇尚健康丰腴的审美情趣。

Silk-smashing Paining, by Zhang Xuan (Tang Dynasty, 618-907)

This painting *Silk-smashing Painting* depicted the working scene of noble women smashing silk and sewing clothes. Due to different identities, ages and works, they acted variant movements and expressions. It was remarkably true to life and reflected the aesthetic taste of pursuing healthy and well-rounded figure in the blooming Tang period.

中唐时期成绩最卓著的诗人要数"诗魔"白居易（772—846）。他的诗通俗易懂，深受民众喜爱，代表作有《长恨歌》《琵琶行》。

Da) by Gao Shi, etc. In the blooming Tang period, men of talent came out in succession, who together created the magnificent "Blooming Tang Grandeur" and inspired the later poets.

The most prestigious poet in the middle Tang period was the "Poetry Wizard", Bai Juyi (772-846), whose poems were easy to understand and well accepted by common people, including *Song of Eternal Sorrow* (*Changhen Ge*)

- 敦煌壁画《反弹琵琶图》（唐）

Mural of Dunhuang *Playing Pear-shaped Lute (Pipa) in the Reverse Way* (Tang Dynasty, 618-907)

• 越窑青瓷莲花碗（唐）
Yue Kiln celadon Porcelain Lotus Petal Bowl (Tang Dynasty, 618-907)

其他如孟郊的《游子吟》、李贺的《苏小小墓》等，都为脍炙人口的名篇。但中唐时期唐诗已现颓势，受朝廷腐败、国力衰退等客观条件影响，中唐诗歌难再有雄壮之美，逐渐出现颓靡消极之音。不过中唐诗风的转变为唐诗开辟了另一种境界，并且成为后世宋诗重理趣的先声。

晚唐时期著名的诗人主要有李商隐、杜牧、温庭筠等。他们为走向衰落的唐诗带来了最后的辉煌。李商隐数篇《无题》都是感人至深、广为传诵的佳作。杜牧的怀古诗更是一绝，其《赤壁怀古》是怀

and *Song of the Lute Player* (*Pipa Xing*). Others like *A Song of the Travelling Son* (*Youzi Yin*) by Meng Jiao, *Tomb of Su Xiaoxiao* (*Su Xiaoxiao Mu*) by Li He, etc., were the famous masterpieces. However, Tang poetry had started to appear its declining tendency. Affected by the corruption of the courtyard, deterioration of the national power and other objective conditions, the poetry of middle Tang period started to play the dejected and passive sound instead of regaining its past grandeur. But the transformation of the poetry style during this period of time opened up another realm which became the first sign of the preference to reasons in poetry-writing in the Song Dynasty (960-1279).

The famous poets in the late Tang period included Li Shangyin, Du Mu, Wen Tingyun, etc., who brought the final spectacularity of the declining Tang poetry. Many works with the title *Untitled* of Li Shangyin were extremely touching and popular masterpieces. And the past-cherishing poems of Du Mu were extraordinary, like his great works titled *Red Cliff Reminiscence* (*Chibi Huaigu*). Wen Tingyun were skilled in both poem and *Ci*. He got better reputation on his *Ci* and initiated the development of this

璀璨唐诗
Splendid Tang Poetry

古诗中的上乘之作。温庭筠则诗词俱佳,以词取胜,为词这种文体到宋代达到鼎盛开启了先河。唐诗在晚唐时期出现了繁荣,在李商隐、杜牧之后彻底进入低谷期,而词则开始崭露头角。

literary form to its prosperous time in the Song Dynasty. Tang poetry flourished in the late Tang Dynasty, and entered the complete low ebb after Li Shangyin and Du Mu, while *Ci* started to emerge.

• 《调琴啜茗图卷》【局部】周昉(唐)
Painting Scroll of Toning the Quqin and Sipping the Tea (Part), by Zhou Fang(Tang Dynasty, 618-907)

• 釉下褐绿彩荷花纹执壶(唐)
Underglazed Greenish Brown Color Handled Pot with Lotus Pattern (Tang Dynasty, 618-907)

> 唐诗魅力

中国现代著名的思想家、文学家鲁迅先生曾经说过："我以为一切好诗,到唐已被做完……"从中不难看出唐诗在人们心目中的地位有多高。从唐朝及以后各朝各代,直到今天的中国人都吟诵唐诗,甚至连几岁的儿童也都能吟咏出几首简单的唐诗。

唐诗不仅在国内地位举足轻重,还在唐朝时就已经流传到日本和朝鲜等东亚诸国,并且为那里的国王、达官显贵、僧侣文人等所青睐。他们也学习汉字、踊跃写诗,并且以李白、杜甫、白居易等唐朝诗人为偶像。各国也先后出现了许多著名的诗人,他们的作品中都保留了很浓厚的唐诗神韵。在古代

> Glamour of Tang Poetry

The famous Chinese modern philosopher and writer, Lu Xun once said,"I think that all the great poems were written in the Tang Dynasty." So we can learn that Tang poetry takes an incomparable position in people's mind. From the Tang Dynasty all the way through the successive later times and even till today, Chinese people often learn to chant Tang poetries. Even for the little kids, they can also recite several simple lines from that.

Not only does Tang poetry have an important status in China, but also was introduced to Japan, Korean peninsula and other countries in East Asia, and was appreciated by their kings, dignitaries, monks and literati. They started to learn Chinese and wrote poems, and worshiped Li Bai, Du Fu, Bai Juyi and other famous

日本，无论是武士还是贵族，都以能写几首汉诗作为自己有修养的象征；僧人们则对白居易的诗歌十分推崇，至今日本还保留着纪念白居易的遗址。日本学者村上哲见在他的《汉诗与日本人》中写道："大唐的诗，如同最美丽的长天，让人只能仰视。"古代朝鲜的李朝皇帝

Chinese poets as their idols. There were many distinguished poets appearing in these countries successively, whose works also preserved obvious features of Tang poetry. In ancient Japan, either samurai or nobleman could write several poems to attest his own accomplishments; monks held the works of Bai Juyi in high esteem. And the site once built for

• 彩色釉陶凤首壶（唐）
Color-glazed Clay Pot with Phoenix Head (Tang Dynasty, 618-907)

自上而下推行汉诗，很多文人名士皆力主写诗要学唐诗，并且身体力行，以杜甫忧国忧民的现实主义诗风为参照对象。

到了当代，随着中国的改革开放，对外文化交流不断深化，唐诗也越来越受到世界的关注，得到了外国读者们的喜爱。在日本现代社会，唐诗仍然有着崇高的地位。许多有地位的日本人仍然以书法撰写唐诗名句，装裱之后挂于办公室

commemorating him is still reserved until now. The Japanese literati Murakami Tetumi wrote in his book *Chinese Poetry and Japanese*: "The poetry of Tang Empire is like the most beautiful heaven to look up to." Emperors of ancient Korea also promoted Chinese poetry from top to bottom. And many scholars believed Tang poetry was the highest realm of writing poems, so they practiced what they preached and took the realistic poet, Du Fu as their reference.

Nowadays, after China's reform and open to the outside world and more communication with foreign countries, Tang poetry captured more and more attention by the world and was appreciated by the foreign readers. In the modern society of Japan, Tang poetry has sublime status as before. Many celebrities still use Chinese brush to write famous poetry lines. They will frame their works

- 《唐人诗意图》杨晋（清）
  Poetic Paining of Tang Dynasty, by Yang Jin (Qing Dynasty, 1616-1911)

或者私人住所，以显示其高雅的品位，甚至连大阪的糕点盒上都印有"霜叶红于二月花"这句唐诗。在最早开始研究中国的欧洲，法国人对唐诗也充满着不衰的探索热情，各国都对研究唐诗产生了浓厚的兴趣，二战后以唐诗为代表的唐代文学在美国甚至发展成为一门显学。美国哈佛大学著名的汉学家斯蒂芬·欧文（Stephen Owen，中文名字

and hang them in the office or private residence to exhibit their elegant taste. Even the cake boxes in Osaka are printed with the famous line of Tang poetry, "The frosted red maple is brighter than the spring flower". In Europe, where people studied China at the earliest time, the French were also full of the constant enthusiasm on exploring Tang poetry. Many countries became interested on the research of it. After the World War

- 彩色釉陶骑马女俑（唐）
  Color-Glazed Clay Statue of a Riding Horse Woman (Tang Dynasty, 618-907)

• 青釉褐绿彩狮座诗文瓷枕（唐）
Green-glazed Greenish Brown Porcelain Pillow with Lion Pedestal and Poem Inscription (Tang Dynasty, 618-907)

文所安）折服于唐诗的魅力，写了大量关于唐诗研究的著作。

在中国国内，唐诗仍有大批忠实的拥趸。人们依然以唐诗作为高雅的象征，使用唐诗名句来表达自己的观点看法和思想感情成为一个人较高综合素质的体现。

唐诗的成就登峰造极，非只言片语可以总结概括。这是有唐一代的精神文化产物，诗中有情，诗中有景，诗中有思，诗中有理，人们的每一种情感都能从诗中找到共鸣，通过诗句恰如其分地表达出

Two, the literature of the Tang Dynasty represented by Tang poetry even was developed into a significant study in America. The famous Sinologist of Harvard University, Stephen Owen (Chinese name: Yuwen Suo'an) not only was subdued to the charm of it, but also wrote many works on the research of Tang poetry.

In China, Tang poetry was still well-accepted by many loyal lovers. People consider it as the symbol of elegance as usual. Reciting famous lines of Tang poetry to express people's own thoughts and emotions now has become the

来。唐朝的政治、经济、历史、风土民俗、社会人物百态都在唐诗中得以体现，唐诗就是一本最生动的历史百科书。多元的哲学思想在唐诗中交相呼应，不同的世界观、人生观和价值观在唐诗中纵横驰骋，生老病死、悲欢离合的感情在唐诗中融合交织。借助诗人们高超的艺术技巧，唐诗名垂千古，经典永恒。

reflection of their high comprehensive quality.

The achievement of Tang poetry has reached the peak of perfection and simply cannot be summed up by several words. It is a spiritual cultural product of the Tang Dynasty, with emotion, landscape, thoughts and philosophy between the lines. Every kind of emotion of human beings can be found in Tang poetry and is expressed appropriately through the lines. The politics, economy, history, folk customs and people in that society are reflected in it. Tang poetry itself is a book of vivid history encyclopedia. Diversified philosophies echo each other in poems; different outlooks on world, life and value gallop within the lines; Life and death, vicissitude of emotions are mingled all together. With the aid of the poets' skillful artistry, Tang poetry has an everlasting name in the history and becomes an eternal classic.

唐诗知识
Knowledge of Tang Poetry

　　无论是用古体诗还是近体诗，都是诗歌中的集大成者，尤其配以题材广泛的诗歌内容，更是巧夺天工的完美组合。诗人们在创作时也在自觉探讨诗歌创作的理论和方法，自由形成的各种流派促进了唐诗的多元化发展，极大地丰富了唐诗的内涵。本部分主要介绍这些有关唐诗的知识，包括唐诗的形式、内容和流派等。阅读这些可以对唐诗有进一步的了解，对于鉴赏唐诗有很大的帮助。

Either the ancient genre poetry or the new genre poetry, is the essence of poetry. Especially accompanying with the rich themes of the poems, it makes the perfect combination. During their writings, poets spontaneously explored the theory and method of poetry writing. The self-formed various schools promoted the diversity of Tang poetry and also enriched its connotation. This part mainly introduced some specialized knowledge, including the forms, contents and schools of Tang poetry, which can help the reader get a further understanding on the poetry itself and its appreciation.

> 唐诗的体裁

唐诗的诗体主要为古体和近体。唐朝诗人在继承古体创作的同时开拓创新，积极推广使用近体写诗，成就了近体诗的艺术升华。

古体诗

顾名思义，古体诗就是按照唐朝以前古代的写诗方法写的诗，诗歌形式比较自由，没有字数、音律、格式等的限制。一首诗里，诗句的字数可以是四个字、五个字、七个字，一般称为"四言体""五言体""七言体"，还有的一首诗里各句字数长短相杂，参差不齐，称为"杂言体"。每首诗的诗句数量也没有特别的限制。四言体古诗，远在《诗经》时代就已被人们

> Genres of Tang Poetry

Tang poetry is mainly divided into ancient and new genres. The poets in the Tang Dynasty inherited the writing of ancient poetry and also developed the new poetry which was actively promoted and finally achieved the artistic sublimation of the new genre.

Ancient Genre Poetry

As its name implies, ancient genre poetry is the poems written according to the methods of the successive dynasties before the Tang Dynasty, with relatively free style and without the limitation in the number of characters, rhyme and pattern. In one poem, the number of characters in all these lines could be varied from four, five or seven, which were relatively called "four-character style", "five-

采用了，到唐代已经逐渐衰微，很少有人再写，唐代的古体诗以五言、七言和杂言为主。

春 思

燕草如碧丝，秦桑低绿枝。
当君怀归日，是妾断肠时。
春风不相识，何事入罗帏？

李白的《春思》是一首五言古诗，描写了一位少妇思念在远方戍

• 《修竹仕女图》仇英（明）
Painting of Maids and Slender Bamboos, by Qiu Ying (Ming Dynasty, 1368-1644)

character style" and "seven-character style". And for those with various numbers of characters in each line within one poem, it was called "blend character style". The number of lines of one poem was also without any specific limitation. The four-character poetry was adopted as far as the era of *The Book of Songs*, and was on the wane by the Tang Dynasty. Few people had ever written it. The ancient poetry of the Tang Dynasty was mainly the five-character, seven-character and blend character.

Spring Yearning

When the Yan's grasses are like tufts of green silk,
And the flourishing mulberry leaves of Qin bend the branches.
As thou think of the day when thou wouldst return from frontier,
I am pining away with a broken heart at home.
The spring breeze is a stranger unknown to me;
What hast it to do with blowing into my silk curtain?

The *Spring Yearning* of Li Bai is a five-character ancient poetry, depicting a young lady missing her husband who was guarded at the frontier far away from the home. It expressed the missing thoughts via the description of the spring scene, which was finely described and fairly touching. The general idea is: The grasses of the Yan area (present northern area of Hebei and Liaoning Provinces, once the frontier) are just as green as tufts of silk and the prosperous mulberry leaves of Qin area (present Shaanxi Province, her husband's hometown) has already bended the branches. My dear husband, when you are homesick at the frontier, I am missing you with a broken heart at home. The amorous spring breeze is a total stranger to me. Why do you blow into my silk curtain and disturb my thoughts?

New Genre Poetry

The new genre poetry, also called "present poetry" or "*Gelv* poetry", is a new poetry style formed in the Tang Dynasty. According to the poets' continuous efforts, constant innovations and frequent appliance and practices, it became a significant poetry genre in the Tang Dynasty, which was used in half of the verses written in that period of time and enriched the creative styles of Tang poetry. Different from the freedom of the ancient genre, the new genre emphasized the symmetry and balance of the poems, in which the number of lines, the number

• 青瓷武士俑（唐）
Celadon Porcelain Warrior Statue (Tang Dynasty, 618-907)

边的丈夫。全诗以景寄情，刻画细腻，委婉动人。诗中大意是：燕塞（今河北北部及辽宁一带，当年是戍边之地）的春草才嫩得像碧绿的小丝，秦地（今陕西一带，征夫们的家乡）的桑叶早已茂密得压弯树枝。郎君啊，当你在边境想家时，正是我在家想你肝肠寸断的日子。多情的春风，我与你素不相识，你为何闯入罗帏，搅乱我的情思？

近体诗

近体诗又叫"今体诗"或"格律诗",是唐代形成的新诗体。经过唐朝诗人的不懈努力、不断创新以及主动用近体诗来创作的自觉,近体诗在唐朝成为一种非常重要的诗体,丰富了唐诗创作的形式。与古体诗的自由完全不同,近体诗讲究对称和均衡,近体诗中诗句的句数,每个分句的字数,字句的音调、音律都有严格的限制。

静夜思

床前明月光,疑是地上霜。
举头望明月,低头思故乡。

of the characters in each line, the tones and rhymes were all strictly determined.

Thoughts on a Tranquil Night
The moon casts a bright light in front of my camp chair,
And I start to wonder if it's frost on ground.
Raising my head, I look at the bright moon;
While bowing, I'm drowned in my nostalgia.

Thoughts on a Tranquil Night, by Li Bai is a five-character *Jueju* (a poem of four lines), having four lines and five characters in each one. Each character's tone in the four lines was arranged according to the fixed regulation of new poetry. The vowels (called *Yunmu* in Chinese syllable) of the last characters in the first, second and fourth lines were kept the same as "ang", which is called "rhyme". In the two clauses of each sentence, the characters or phrases at the same position must correspond to each other, for example, "raising head" and "bowing" are actions of head; "look" and "be drowned" are verbs leading the latter

- 《静夜思》诗意图
  Poetic Painting of *Thoughts on a Tranquil Night*

李白的《静夜思》是一首五言绝句，全诗一共4个分句，每个分句5个字，每个分句里的每个字的音调都按照近体诗的固定规则安排。最后一个字的元音部分（汉语拼音中叫韵母）在第一、第二、第四个分句中保持一致，都是ang，这种现象叫作"押韵"。每句话的两个分句中，相同位置的字或词要有一定的对应关系，比如"举头"和"低头"都是关于头的动作，"望"和"思"都是动词，统领后面的名词"明月"和"故乡"。这是对仗。而每句诗里的每个字的音调都有固定的规则要遵守，与中国现代汉语拼音的四个声调的变化类似，仿佛是在一首固定的乐谱里填词一样，只是这个规则并不是教条和不容更改的。

正是因为近体诗具有这些特点，读起来工整顺口，富有一定的音乐性，更适合诗歌内容和感情的表达，所以发展迅速，逐渐取代了古体诗在诗坛的地位，成为唐代及唐代以后的主要诗体。后代诗人都广泛地使用近体诗进行创作，奠定了近体诗在中国诗歌史中的重要地位。李白、杜甫、李商隐等都是近体诗的集大成者。

nouns "bright moon" and "nostalgia". It's called antithesis. And the tones of each character in every line should follow the determined rules. Resembling the four tonetic variations of modern Chinese Pinyin, it seems like writing lyric for a fixed music score. And its regulations and rules are not doctrinal and unchangeable.

Because of these features of the new genre poetry, it is easily read and full of rhythm, which is more appropriate for the expressions of the contents and emotions. So it was rapidly developed and gradually replaced the position of the ancient poetry, becoming the main poetry style in and after the Tang Dynasty. The later poets widely applied the new genre to write verses, which built its significant

• 白釉灯台（唐）
White-glazed Lampstand (Tang Dynasty, 618-907)

近体诗主要分为律诗和绝句。按照每句五个字和每句七个字的分类，律诗主要分为五言律诗和七言律诗；绝句也主要分为五言绝句和七言绝句，简称"五绝"和"七绝"。律诗一般是八句，而绝句一般是四句。从形式上看，绝句短小精悍，只有律诗一半的容量，而写出来的艺术水平却丝毫不亚于律诗。

李白、王昌龄都是写绝句的高手，而杜甫则是律诗中的王者，是七言律诗最高艺术成就的代表。

律诗

律诗的第一、第二句称为"首联"，第三、第四句为"颔联"，第五、第六句为"颈联"，第七、第八句为"尾联"。按照规定，"颔联"和"颈联"必须对仗；第二、第四、第六、第八句最后的一个字必须同韵。

旅夜书怀

细草微风岸，危樯独夜舟。
星垂平野阔，月涌大江流。
名岂文章著，官应老病休。
飘飘何所似？天地一沙鸥。

status in the history of Chinese poetry. Li Bai, Du Fu, Li Shangyin, and other poets were the masters of new genre poetry.

The new genre poetry mainly includes *Lvshi* (a poem of eight lines) and *Jueju* (a poem of four lines). According to the number of the characters in each line, it also can be divided into five-character and seven-character. So *Lvshi* has five-character *Lvshi* and seven-character *Lvshi*; and *Jueju* has five-character *Jueju* and seven-character *Jueju*, or the shortened form "five-*Jue*" and "seven-*Jue*". *Lvshi* usually has eight lines and *Jueju* is with four lines. In terms of the form, *Jueju* is short and concise, which only has half information of *Lvshi*, however they possess equal artistry in all the aspects.

Li Bai and Wang Changling were skillful poets of *Jueju*, while Du Fu was the king of *Lvshi*, who represented the highest artistic achievement of *Lvshi*.

Lvshi (a poem of eight lines)

In *Lvshi*, the first and second lines are called "head sentence"; the third and fourth lines are "chin sentence"; the fifth and sixth lines are "neck sentence"; and the seventh and eighth lines are "tail

诗意：微风吹拂着江岸的细草，小船在夜里孤独地停泊着。星星远在天边显得原野更加宽阔；月光映在江水中随波涌动，大江滚滚东流。我难道只是因为文章而出名吗？或许年老病多也应该辞官了。我四处漂泊就像天地间的一只孤零零的沙鸥。

杜甫的五言律诗《旅夜书怀》首联、颔联和颈联都是对仗的，最后一句则没有，却将整个诗歌的感情提升到另一层境界，可见表达感

sentence". According to the rules, the "head sentence" and "neck sentence" must be written in antithesis; while the last characters of the second, fourth, sixth and eighth lines should be in the same rhyme.

Night Travel Notes

Gentle breeze strokes the tender grass on the bank,
A solitary boat moors in the night with its mast towering aloft.
The stars are hanging in the sky against the vast wilderness,
The moon casts its reflection in the flowing river.
Do I earn my reputation relying on my writings?
Being old and sick, I shall resign from my post.
Wandering in this world, what should I resemble?
Just like a sand gull soaring between heaven and earth.

General idea: The gentle breeze strokes the tender grass on the river bank and the boat moors in the night solitarily.

- 《扁舟傲睨图》佚名（元）
Overlooked Small Boat Painting, by Anonymity (Yuan Dynasty, 1206-1368)

- **四川成都杜甫草堂**

  位于四川成都的杜甫草堂是公元759年杜甫流寓成都时的居所。《旅夜书怀》是杜甫于765年离开成都以后在旅途中所作。

  Du Fu's Humble Cottage in Chengdu City, Sichuan Province

  Situated in Chengdu City, Sichuan Province, Du Fu's humble cottage was his temporary residence when he was stranded in Chengdu. And the famous verse *Night Travel Notes* was written in his trip after he left Chengdu in 765.

情、描述景物的时候需变换格式。这既遵循了一定的规律，又符合了起承转合的情绪变化曲线，将内容充分表达且恰到好处，提高了整首诗歌的艺术水平。律诗创作是一种富有技术含量的创作挑战，而唐朝诗人能在这种框架下创作出无数精妙绝伦的作品，其艺术水平之高超、才能之卓越显而易见。

The stars hanging in the sky make the wilderness look broader. The moonlight cast in the river is flowing with the water waves. Do I only earn my reputation on my writings? Or maybe I am old and sick now, so I should resign from my post. I wander around just like a sand gull flying between heaven and earth.

　　Except for the tail sentence, the head, chin and neck sentences of the *Night Travel Notes* by Du Fu were all written in antithesis, which raised the emotion in this verse to another level of realm. It's obvious that the transformation of the patterns when expressing feelings and depicting scenes could make the content conveyed more appropriately and also raise the whole verse's artistic standard. So the writing of *Lvshi* is a skillful challenge. And poets of the Tang Dynasty could write so many fascinating masterpieces under this frame, which is definitely a reflection of their excellence.

绝句

绝句在形式上看似律诗的一半，其实并不是截取自律诗，而是从古体诗中进化而来的一种诗体。但它的形式却遵循近体诗的诗体，和律诗一样遵守音调、对仗、押韵等规则。

早发白帝城

朝辞白帝彩云间，千里江陵一日还。
两岸猿声啼不住，轻舟已过万重山。

诗意：清晨的白帝城云雾缭绕，仿佛在彩云之间，我离开白帝

Jueju (a Poem of Four Lines)

In terms of the form, *Jueju* seems like a half *Lvshi*. Actually, instead of being cut out from *Lvshi*, it's a poetry style evolved from the ancient poetry with a form followed the new genre and the same rules on the tones, antithesis and rhymes like *Lvshi*.

Sailing Early From Baidi Town

We set sail at dawn from Baidi Town under a rosy sky,
On thousand-mile trip down to Jiangling within one day.
The noisy chatter of apes from the shores followed us all the way.
Lightly, our boat has skipped past ten thousand green mountains.

General idea: The Baidi Town is bemisted in the early morning, which seems to be surrounded by colorful clouds. I'm leaving for Jiangling today. Though the trip is as far as thousand miles away, we'll arrive there just within

- 《早发白帝城》诗意图
  Poetic Painting of *Sailing Early From Baidi Town*

城去江陵。虽然千里之遥，乘船只用一天时间就已经到达那里。江河的两岸传来猿猴的啼声，回荡不绝。声音还没有消失，轻快的小船已驶过连绵不断的层峦叠嶂。

这是李白最著名的七言绝句之一。在吟咏七绝的时候，按照相同的节奏来停顿，第三分句的声调自然上扬，而第四分句的音调又降了下来，仿佛置身于诗人在群峰高耸的山涧中坐船渡江所体会到的空灵之感中。此诗读起来就好像交响乐曲，感觉上有激昂也有舒缓，有高音也有低音。这就是近体诗的魅力之所在，看似工整，又具有一定的变化，随着诗人在文字上的精心编排，产生了唯美的艺术效果，令读诗和写诗的人的心灵都体验到了唯美奇妙的艺术享受。

one day by boat. The cries of apes from the shores followed us all the way. And the little boat has passed those continuous mountains swiftly.

This is one of the famous seven-character *Jueju* of Li Bai. When chanting seven-*Jue*, it should pause at the same tempo. The tone of the third line should rise up, while the tone of the fourth line should go down, as if sitting on the sailing boat in the mountain creek and feeling the intangible sensation of the poet. This verse is just like a piece of symphony, exciting and leisurely, with high pitch as well as the low pitch. It is the charm of the new genre poetry, which seems to be neat, yet having some variations. With the delicate arrangement of the characters by the poet, it exhibits an artistic effect, making both the reader and writer experience a wonderful artistic feast.

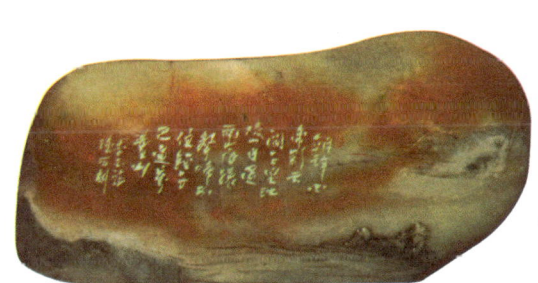

• 青田石摆件"朝辞白帝城"
  Qingtian Adornment with the Theme of *Sailing Early From Baidi Town*

> 唐诗的题材

唐诗的内容丰富多彩、包罗万象，人们所能想到的各个方面、各个层次的内容都有涉猎，其中也包含了人们复杂多变的内心情感。后人可以通过唐诗来考察当时的社会生活，甚至还能从中分析出几千年前古人的思想性格和感情寄托。唐代诗人创作如同现代人拍照、写日记一样，将自己眼中的唐朝的点点滴滴都保留在了唐诗中，让后人可以想象出当时的情景，体会唐朝的韵味。然而，读过很多唐诗之后，就会发现在上万首唐诗里面，对于同一时间、同一事件或同一事物，因为诗人的想法和视角的不同，所反映出的状态和面貌也不

> Themes of Tang Poetry

The content of Tang poetry is full of variety, including all the aspects that people could ever imagined, as well as human's complicated emotions deep inside. The descendants can study the social lives of that period of time through Tang poetry, even analyzing ancient people's thoughts and feelings thousands of years ago. The poetry-writing in the Tang Dynasty functioned as same as the modern photograph and diary. They recorded every little part of their lives in the poetry, so the descendants can image the scenes of that time and experience the charm of the Tang Dynasty. However, after reading abundant Tang poetry, one will find that regarding the same time, same event or same object, there are different reflections and appearances

同。比如秋天，有的诗人到了秋天就情不自禁写出悲伤哀叹的诗句，而有的诗人却赞颂秋天，用 created by the tens of thousands verses due to the variety of poets' thoughts and point of views. For example, referring to autumn, some couldn't help themselves to write down the sad and bitter lines, while some might praise and express their joy and happiness via verses. The theme as the season autumn is their only identical point. So even if the poetries were varied from one another and with their own features respectively, people are still used to classifying poems on themes as which, ranging from scene-description, narration, history-recording or object-depicting, all of which are the incentive triggering poets' mood fluctuations. After all, the writers just wanted to deliver their own thoughts, and express their personal emotions.

- 《秋山图轴》朱耷（清）
  Scroll Painting of Autumn Mountains, by Zhu Da (Qing Dynasty, 1616-1911)

诗句表达愉悦的心情，他们唯一相同之处是都将关注点放在秋天这个季节上。因此尽管诗歌作品风格迥异、各具特色，人们都习惯以唐诗中的内容主题来归纳分类。因为不管写景、叙事、咏史、咏物，都是引发诗人情绪、做出反应的诱因。归根结底，诗人都是想要表达自我精神世界的思想，抒发个人的情怀。

写景（抒情）诗

　　唐朝版图辽阔，风景秀丽，唐人酷爱游山玩水，漫游是唐朝诗人生活的一个非常重要的组成部分。不管是江南的青山秀水，还是北方的大漠孤烟，不管是巴蜀的崇山峻岭，还是长江的烟雨楼台，全都被诗人写入诗中。而诗人们在看见壮丽山河之后内心不禁产生了无限的感情，或喜，或悲，或愁，或闷，这些情绪都融入他们写景的诗句当中，产生了情景交融的绝妙效果，于是写景（抒情）诗就出现了。

　　崔颢（约704—754）的《黄鹤楼》就是一首典型的写景（抒情）诗，描写的是中国四大名楼之一黄

Landscape (Emotion-expressing) Poetry

China owned a broad territory with beautiful landscape in the Tang Dynasty. The people were fond of traveling among the mountains and rivers, which was an important part of their lives. Both the graceful scenery of the south of Yangtze River, and the expansive desert of the north areas; both the steep cliffs of Ba-Shu (two ancient cities in Sichuan), and the pavilions and terraces in the valley of Yangtze River, were all recorded in the poems. And the affections generated after the poets seeing all these magnificent landscapes, being happy, sad, worried, or depressed, were all blended in those lines, which produced an excellent fusion of emotions and scenes. So the landscape (emotion-expressing) poetry was born.

Yellow Crane Tower, by Cui Hao (approx. 704-754) is a typical landscape (emotion-expressing) poetry, describing the scenery of Yellow Crane Tower, one of the Four Great Towers of China. The poet was inspired by the splendid landscape and plumped out the verse at one stretch. Allegedly, after reading this, even "Poetry Immortal" Li Bai dropped his writing brush and felt ashamed to

鹤楼的风景，诗人即景生情，诗兴大发，脱口而出，一气呵成。传说连"诗仙"李白看到《黄鹤楼》之后都自愧不如，随即搁笔。

黄鹤楼

昔人已乘黄鹤去，此地空余黄鹤楼。
黄鹤一去不复返，白云千载空悠悠。
晴川历历汉阳树，芳草萋萋鹦鹉洲。
日暮乡关何处是？烟波江上使人愁。

诗意：传说中的仙人已乘黄鹤飞去，此处只留下空荡荡的黄鹤楼。飞走的黄鹤再也没有回来，唯

write a new verse beside Cui Hao's masterpiece.

Yellow Crane Tower

An ancient saint has ridden a yellow crane and flew away,
And here is left only a Yellow Crane Tower.
The yellow crane has left and will not return,
Only the white clouds float in sky for a thousand years.
Distinct rows of trees grow along the creek in Hanyang,
And the green grass is flourishing on Parrot Isle.
Where is my hometown in this approaching evening?
The haze on the river makes me grieve and pine.

General idea: The legendary sage has ridden a yellow crane and flew away. Only the empty Yellow Crane Tower was left at the place. The yellow crane will never come back. And only the white clouds have never changed for a

● 云鹤纹玉饰（宋）
鹤是中国稀有的珍禽，古来被视为长寿的象征。
Jade Adornment with Pattern of Clouds and Cranes (Song Dynasty, 960-1279)
Crane is a rare bird in China and has been considered as the symbol of longevity since the ancient times.

● 湖北武汉黄鹤楼（图片提供：全景正片）

黄鹤楼位于湖北省武汉市蛇山的黄鹤矶头，面对鹦鹉洲，与湖南岳阳楼、江西滕王阁、山东蓬莱阁合称"中国四大名楼"，有"天下江山第一楼"之誉。相传始建于三国时期，历代屡毁屡建，现楼为1981年重建。

Yellow Crane Tower in Wuhan City, Hubei Province

The Yellow Crane Tower is situated at the Yellow Crane Rock (Jitou, rock on the river shore) of the Mount Snake in Wuhan City, Hubei Province, facing the Parrot Isle, which possesses the reputation as "The Greatest Tower in the World" and together with Yueyang Tower in Hunan Province, Pavilion of Prince Teng in Jiangxi Province, Penglai Taoist Temple in Shandong Province, are called "Four Great Towers of China". It's said it was built in the Three Kingdoms Period (220-280) and being destroyed and repaired for several times during the successive dynasties. The present tower was rebuilt in 1981.

有悠悠白云千年依旧。阳光照耀下的汉阳树木清晰可见，鹦鹉洲的芳草长得郁郁葱葱。眺望远方，天色已晚，故乡在哪儿呢？眼前只见一片雾霭笼罩江面，给人带来深深的愁绪。

thousand years. Bathed in the sunshine, the trees of Hanyang can be seen clearly. And the green grass on the Parrot Isle is flourishing now. Looking into the distance, the evening is about to come. However, where is my hometown? I can only see the haze on the river, which really makes me grieve and pine.

叙事（咏怀）诗

唐人写诗经常信手拈来，生活中的奇闻趣事，哪怕是微不足道的小事都可以入诗。然而这并不是单纯的记录，而是通过写事来表达自身的思想感情：对于社会现实的感悟，对于人生价值的思考，对于济世理想的追求。借讲述事情来表明志向、抒发感情、慨叹命运是唐朝诗人普遍使用的表达方式。杜甫的《石壕吏》就是最典型的代表。

石壕吏

暮投石壕村，有吏夜捉人。
老翁逾墙走，老妇出门看。
吏呼一何怒！妇啼一何苦！
听妇前致词：三男邺城戍。
一男附书至，二男新战死。
存者且偷生，死者长已矣！
室中更无人，惟有乳下孙。
有孙母未去，出入无完裙。
老妪力虽衰，请从吏夜归。
急应河阳役，犹得备晨炊。
夜久语声绝，如闻泣幽咽。
天明登前途，独与老翁别。

Narrative (Feeling-expressing) Poetry

People in the Tang Dynasty wrote poems freely without too much hesitation. They were ready to include in poems any news and anecdotes in life, and even the most trivial incidents. However, it was not a mere recording; rather, the poet did so to display his thoughts and feelings: how he brooded over social realities, how he pondered on the values of life, and how he pursued his ideal to serve the world. It was common practice for poets in the Tang Dynasty to demonstrate aspirations, express emotions and grieve over destinies through telling narrative stories. Du Fu's *The Pressgang at Stone Moat Village* is a typical example.

The Pressgang at Stone Moat Village

I seek for shelter at nightfall.
The pressgang is coming.
My old host climbs over the wall;
My old hostess answers the door.
The sergeant shouts angrily!
The woman cries bitterly!
I hear what she tries to explain:
"I had three sons guarding the town Ye.
One wrote a letter telling me
That his brothers were killed in war.
He'll keep alive if he can be;

- **唐代明光铠复原图**

  明光铠是魏晋至唐代流行的武将铠甲，其前身和背后有圆形护心镜，大多以铜、铁等金属制成，并且打磨得极光，在太阳照射下会发出耀眼的"明光"，因而得名。

  Restitute Picture of Bright Shining (*Mingguang*) Armour (Tang Dynasty, 618-907)

  Bright Shining Armour was a suit of armour popular since the Three Kingdoms Period (220-280), through the Southern and Northern dynasties (420-589), to the Tang Dynasty. It had a breastplate and a backplate, both round, to protect the heart. They were usually made of metals like copper and iron and were finely polished to achieve a brilliant gloss in sunshine, hence *Mingguang*, meaning bright shining.

诗意：（我）傍晚投宿石壕村，官差半夜来村里抓壮丁。老头儿越墙逃走，他的老伴出来见人。官差吼得非常凶狠！老妇人啼哭得非常可怜！老妇对官差说："我的三个儿子都在邺城军中服役，其中一个儿子捎信回来，说另两个儿子

The dead have passed and are no more.
In the house there is no man left,
Except for my grandson in the cradle.
His mother hasn't got remarried,
She can't come out, in tatters dressed.
Though I'm a woman weak and old,
I beg to go tonight with you,
That I may serve in the stronghold in Heyang
And cook morning meals as my due."
Late at night, the noisy fades away;
I still seem to hear sob and sigh.
At dawn again I set out on my journey
And only bid farewell to my host.

General idea: Toward evening, the poet seeks shelter in the Stone Moat Village. At midnight, a sergeant comes to search for able-bodied men for the army, upon which the old host climbs over the wall and flees, and his wife goes to answer the door. The ferocious sergeant shouts the poor hostess into desperate cry. She says to the sergeant: "I had three sons serving in the army in town Ye. Then one wrote saying that the other two were killed recently. Those who are alive, though miserable, can at least make a living; yet those who are dead would never revive! Here is only an infant boy in my family, whose mother has not yet remarried. She doesn't even have a single

最近刚刚战死。活着的人姑且活一天算一天，死去的人永远不会复生了！家里只有个还没断奶的孙儿，他的母亲还没有改嫁，她连一件可以穿出去见人的好衣服都没有。老妇我虽然年老体衰，请让我跟你们连夜赶回军营去，及时到河阳服役，还来得及为军队准备早餐。"夜深了，嘈杂的声音消失了，隐约还能听到低微断续的哭声。（我）天亮赶路，只能和老头儿一个人告别了。

全诗通过描述作者亲眼所见的石壕吏乘夜捉人充军的经过，反映了当时唐朝政府因为"安史之乱"而疯狂征兵，导致民不聊生、妻离子散的悲惨现状，控诉战争给民众带来的深重苦难，表达了诗人对百姓的深切同情。

piece of clothing neat enough to dress in public. I, an old woman, though senile and weak, plead that you take me to the stronghold in Heyang overnight so I can make breakfast for the soldiers before it's too late." The night growing late, the noises fade away, but the poet still hears continuous weep. At dawn, the poet has to resume his journey and bids farewell only to the old host.

The poem depicted how the pressgang at Stone Moat Village captured villagers for the army at night, which the poet witnessed. Through this, it revealed that after An-Shi Rebellion (755-763), the Tang government recruited soldiers badly, leaving people suffering from poverty and broken families. Thus, the poem accused war of its introduction of untold miseries and exhibited the poet's sympathy toward the suffering people.

- 青瓷持刀男俑（唐）
  Celadon Porcelain Statue of a Man with a Sword (Tang Dynasty, 618-907)

咏史（怀古）诗

　　中国古代非常注重对历史的记录和考察，唐朝也不例外。诗人可以通过各种途径了解古代的历史。那些具有传奇色彩、举世闻名的历史名人、名胜古迹更加受到追捧和爱戴。咏史（怀古）诗就是以历史事件、历史人物、历史遗迹为题材的诗歌。诗人通过追忆历史，祭奠古迹来寄托哀思，通过历史的教训来影射讽刺当代的社会现实，以古鉴今，又或者通过古今穿越的对比

● 四川成都武侯祠
Temple of Marquis in Chengdu City, Sichuan Province

Historical (Past-cherishing) Poetry

Ancient Chinese stressed importance of recording and studying history, so did people in the Tang Dynasty. Poets acquainted themselves with history in many ways, especially through visiting and adoring the legendary and well-known sites of historical figures and events. Historical (past-cherishing) poetry is the poem that addresses the themes of historical events, figures and relics. Poets either mourned the ancients through recalling historical events and visiting historical sites; or, alluded to or satirized contemporary social realities through drawing lessons from history; or, implicitly expressed his innermost thoughts through comparing different ages.

　　Historical (past-cherishing) poetry shares contents and ideas more profound than those of other schools of Tang poetry. For Chinese, the long history of thousands of years is, besides a treasure, a heavy burden. So heavy that poets tended to relate their own fates to ancient people when visiting relics and memorizing predecessors. Believing that they would be part of history, they wondered how their posterity would think

和映衬来含蓄表达内心真实的观点和看法。

在各种题材的唐诗中，咏史诗的内容与思想都相对比较沉重。中国几千年积淀的历史是一笔财富，也是沉重的负担，以至于诗人们在凭吊古迹、追忆古人的时候，常常联想到自身的命运。在未来他们也将成为历史，后人又会如何评价他们呢？不禁发出对古人成就地位的慨叹，抒发对于历史不再、物换星移、物是人非的悲哀之情。杜甫的《蜀相》就是最有名的咏史诗，他借诸葛亮来慨叹自身的命运，感情基调深沉厚重。

蜀　相

丞相祠堂何处寻？锦官城外柏森森。
映阶碧草自春色，隔叶黄鹂空好音。
三顾频烦天下计，两朝开济老臣心。
出师未捷身先死，长使英雄泪满襟。

诗意：三国时蜀汉丞相诸葛亮的祠堂在哪里？在成都城外那柏树茂密的地方。台阶前的绿草展示着一片春色，树上的黄鹂在婉转地鸣唱。诸葛亮被先主刘备三顾茅庐邀请出山定夺天下，辅佐两朝君主开

of them. Consequently, they could not help but sigh over the achievements and status of ancient people and exhibit their grief over the changing history, the flying time and the deceasing humanity. Du Fu's *Temple of the Premier of Shu* is the most famous historical poem. The poet wrote of Zhuge Liang to deplore his own fate, in a melancholy and sober tone.

Temple of the Premier of Shu

Where is the famous premier's temple to be found?
Outside the Town Jinguan with flourishing cypresses around.
Spring grass grows green and long in front of the steps,
And amid the leaves golden orioles sing their song.
Thrice the king visited him for the State's

• 诸葛亮像
Portrait of Zhuge Liang

•《三顾草庐图轴》戴进（明）
Scroll Painting of Three Visits to the Cottage, by Dai Jin (Ming Dynasty, 1368-1644)

创蜀汉伟业，以尽忠诚老臣之心！可惜出师伐魏还没有成功，他就病亡于军中，这份遗憾让历代英雄们都闻之伤心、泪湿衣襟！

咏物（言志）诗

咏物（言志）诗就是通过对事物的描绘咏叹体现对实现个人理想和价值的向往。咏物诗中所咏之物往往是诗人的化身，因为具备某些自然属性符合诗人对品格的要求，所以被拿来作为主题写诗，达到诗人塑造自我的目的。诗中所咏之物与诗人自身的形象完全融合在一起，成为诗人思想感情的寄托。在诗中，作者或流露出自己的人生态度，或寄寓美好的愿望，或包含生活的哲理，或表现作者的生活情趣。贺知章的《咏柳》吟咏的就是春天的柳树，将心情寄托于有着美好姿态的杨柳之上，洋溢着诗人的愉悦心情。

咏 柳

碧玉妆成一树高，万条垂下绿丝绦。
不知细叶谁裁出，二月春风似剪刀。

future strategy;
He served heart and soul to the kingdom during two reigns.
He died before accomplishing his career,
Which always made heroes wet their sleeves with tear.

General idea: Where is the temple of Zhuge Liang, premier of the Kingdom of Shu-Han (221-263) during the Three Kingdoms Period (220-265)? It is outside the Town of Chengdu, amid the dense cypresses. Before the steps of the temple, grows fresh grass, informing people of the coming spring. And orioles are singing sweet songs in the trees. The first king Liu Bei thrice visited Zhuge Liang, inviting him to serve the country. Zhuge Liang assisted two consecutive kings to expand and make prosperous the Kingdom of Shu-Han, heart and soul. It's a pity that he died in the army before conquering the Kingdom of Wei (220-265). Heroes for generations have been weeping for the undone cause and this distinguished man.

Object-chanting (Ambition-expressing) Poetry

Object-chanting poetry (or ambition-expressing poetry) describes and chants

诗意：如同碧玉装扮而成的高高的柳树，它飘逸的柳条柔嫩轻盈，像许多条绿色的丝带，低垂着，在春风中婆娑起舞。这一片片纤细精巧的柳叶，是谁精心剪裁出来的呢？早春二月的微风，恰似巧夺天工的剪刀，正是它裁剪出了这些别致的柳叶，将垂柳装饰成一道亮丽的风景。

山水田园诗

很多唐朝诗人都有山水田园诗的佳作，这并非山水田园诗派诗人们的专利。但王维、孟浩然等

• 苏州拙政园早春的垂柳
Weeping Willows in Early Spring in Humble Administrator's Garden in Suzhou City

objects to reveal the poets' aspiration to realize their ideals and values. The object chanted in such a poem is often an embodiment of the poet, because the natural attributes of the object are in accordance with the dream attributes the poet asks of a person. When an object like this is chanted, the poet is actually perfecting himself. In the poem, the chanted object entirely fuses with the poet himself and acts as the carrier of the poet's thoughts and feelings. The poet either reveals his attitudes toward life, or embeds pleasant dreams; either discovers philosophy in life, or shows his taste and temperament. He Zhizhang in his poem *The Willow*, chanted willows in Spring, and rested his feelings on the elegant plants. The poet's delightful emotion flows throughout the poem.

The Willow

From a tall tree draped with pieces of green jade,
Like thousands of green silk strips waving and hanging low.
Who cut out these slender leaves so well displayed?
The February spring wind is as sharp as a pair of scissors.

- 贺知章像

贺知章（659—约744），字季真，号四明狂客，唐越州会稽永兴（今浙江杭州市萧山区）人，作诗以绝句见长，风格独特，清新潇洒。

Portrait of He Zhizhang

He Zhizhang (659-approx.744), or Jizhen (courtesy name), self-titled Siming Kuangke (the crazy man named Siming), was a poet in the Tang Dynasty (618-907) born in Yongxing, Kuaiji, Yuezhou (present Xiaoshan District, Hangzhou City, Zhejiang Province.) He was skilled at writing *Jueju* (a poem of four lines), characterized by his fresh and unrestrained style.

General idea: The slender willows, as if decorated with green jades, have strips delicate and light. Like numerous ribbons, they hang low and elegantly dance in the spring breeze. The leaves are slim and graceful, and who could have cut out them? It is the early-spring breeze in February which is like a pair of scissors with divine skill that has cut out these elaborate leaves, making the willows a picturesque scenery.

Landscape and Pastoral Poetry

Many poets in the Tang Dynasty had masterpieces of landscape and pastoral poems, which were not exclusive to poets of the landscape and pastoral poetic school. Nevertheless, poets of this school like Wang Wei and Meng Haoran created the finest landscape poems and boasted more and better pieces than other poets both on quantity and quality. They mainly described natural landscape, rural scenery and serene and reclusive life in the countryside, all artistic in conception, simple yet elegant in style, and fresh in language. It is different from emotion-expressing poetry in that landscape and pastoral poetry attempts to loyally describe the scenery itself and the person involved is only there to enjoy

山水田园诗派诗人创作的作品堪称典范，并且创作的数量和质量都占优。这类诗主要描写自然风光、农村景物，以及安逸恬淡的隐居生活。诗作意境优美，风格淡雅，语言清丽。和写景抒情诗的不同之处在于，山水田园诗更注重客观地还原景物本身，将人置于景物之中去欣赏大自然的美好。而写景抒情诗是透过诗人的视野选取景物，为了表达感情的需要而描述心中的景物，景成为诗人内心的一部分，情中有景，景中有情，这时的景物不一定是接近真实的，而是经过艺术创作加工过的意象。譬如王维的 the splendid nature, whereas emotion-expressing poetry dealt with scenery to serve the poet in expressing his emotions. The scenery became part of the poet's inner world, and emotions and the scenery were united as an organic whole. The scenery in emotion-expressing poetry is more imaginary than actual, with artistic projections. A typical example of landscape and pastoral poetry is Wang Wei's *The Magnolia Village*.

• 《秋山草堂图》王蒙（元）
Cottage in Autumn Hills, by Wang Meng (Yuan Dynasty, 1206-1368)

• 青釉蟠龙罂（唐）
Green-glazed Small-mouthed Jar with a Twining Dragon (Tang Dynasty, 618-907)

《木兰柴》就是一首典型的山水田园诗。

木兰柴

秋山敛余照，飞鸟逐前侣。
彩翠时分明，夕岚无处所。

这首五言绝句描写了傍晚时分天色无光而明的短暂时刻的自然景物，活画出一幅秋山暮霭鸟归图。亮丽的色彩，幽美的境界，像真的图画一样，让人感觉仿佛眼前出现了一幅秋天傍晚大山之中的富有生机而绝美的图画。全诗大意为：秋日的山顶旁的半轮夕阳，还剩下一抹余晖，晚霞的金光映照着山林，增添了秋天山林中斑斓的色彩。鸟儿追逐着它们的伴侣在夕阳下飞回林中巢穴。鲜艳翠绿的山色时时变幻，山林中的雾气朦胧渐稀。

边塞征战诗

边塞征战诗以边塞军旅生活为主要题材，或描写奇异的塞外风光，或反映驻守边境的艰辛，是唐朝诗歌的重要组成部分。根据记载，唐以前各个朝代涉及边塞题材

The Magnolia Village

The sunset glow is quitting the autumn hills,
The birds are flying, chasing with their couples.
From time to time the shiny green is clear,
The evening mist is gradually spread.

This five-character *Jueju* (a poem of four lines) recorded the transient natural scenery toward evening when the world is still light though the sun has set down, thus vividly forming a scene of hills, evening mist and returning birds in autumn. With the bright color and gentle atmosphere, the poem becomes a real picture, presenting before the reader a spectacular view of the lively mountains toward an autumn evening. General idea: In an autumn day, the sun is half set down beyond the hills. The afterglow is shining over the hills, adding gorgeous hues to the autumn forests. The birds, chasing their mates, are flying back to their nests in the fading sunshine. The color of the bright green hills varies in the spilling and hazy vapor.

Frontier Fortress Poetry

Frontier fortress poetry took military life at the frontier fortress as its theme, depicting the exotic scenes beyond the Great Wall or reflecting the soldiers'

的诗歌总和不到200首，而唐朝就有2000多首，可以说边塞征战诗盛于唐朝，也胜在唐朝。这和唐朝的国情有很大的关联，也是边塞诗派的诗人们努力创作的结果。边塞征战诗的特点非常鲜明，深刻地反映出唐朝边境战事的残酷和驻守边关将士们的艰辛苦楚。诗人通过描写恶劣的自然环境，烘托出将士们坚毅勇敢的英雄气质，也对常年生活在这里的百姓抱有深刻的同情。从一个小小的边关缩影就可以看出整个

• 《太行晴雪图》谢时臣（明）
Taihang Mountain in Sunshine after Heavy Snow, by Xie Shichen (Ming Dynasty, 1368-1644)

hardship in the frontier areas, which was an important part of Tang poetry. It was recorded that poems of this theme before the Tang Dynasty totaled less than 200 pieces, whereas over 2,000 were written in the Tang Dynasty alone. As it were, frontier fortress poetry both flourished and reached its peak in the Tang Dynasty. This was mainly benefit by the national conditions of that period as well as the efforts of the frontier fortress poets. It had distinct characteristics, reflecting profoundly the cruel warfare in the frontier areas and the miserable life of frontier soldiers. Through the description of the harsh natural environment, the poets tried to highlight the heroic mettle of the valiant soldiers and also showed their deep sympathy toward the local people. They were like several little epitomes of the ambitions and strength of the Great Tang Empire. Therefore, they were of irreplaceable significance among Tang poetry. Frontier fortress poetry was bold, heroic, stirring, and high-spirited in style, which was well exemplified by the lines in *Seeing Assistant Wu Back to Chang'an in the Snow* written by the famous frontier fortress poet Cen Shen (approx. 715-770): "Like spring wind coming up in the night, blowing

大唐的气势和境况，边塞诗在唐朝诗坛有着无可取代的重要地位。边塞诗的艺术风格高亢豪迈、悲壮昂扬，比如著名的边塞诗人岑参（约715—770）在《白雪歌送武判官归京》中的名句"忽如一夜春风来，千树万树梨花开"，形容边塞的大雪一夜之间将所有事物都裹成白色，挂在树枝上的雪花仿佛开满的梨花一样。诗人用富有浪漫主义色彩的诗句来形容天气的残酷寒冷，境界奇绝，格调高昂，成为千古名句。

白雪歌送武判官归京

北风卷地白草折，胡天八月即飞雪。
忽如一夜春风来，千树万树梨花开。
散入珠帘湿罗幕，狐裘不暖锦衾薄。
将军角弓不得控，都护铁衣冷难着。
瀚海阑干百丈冰，愁云惨淡万里凝。
中军置酒饮归客，胡琴琵琶与羌笛。
纷纷暮雪下辕门，风掣红旗冻不翻。
轮台东门送君去，去时雪满天山路。
山回路转不见君，雪上空留马行处。

此诗在边塞诗中难得色彩瑰丽浪漫，气势浑然磅礴，堪称盛唐时期边塞诗的压卷之作。全文的意

open the petals of ten thousand pear-trees." Overnight, the heavy snow in the frontier fortress lays a white cloth over everything, and seems like pear blossoms when falling on the tree branches. The fiercely cold weather was described in romantic verse which because of its marvelous and majestic depiction, has been adored up till now.

Seeing Assistant Wu Back to Chang'an in the Snow
The north wind rolled the sere grasses and broke them,
In August, snow was already across the Tartar sky.
Like spring wind coming up in the night,
Blowing open the petals of ten thousand pear-trees.
It entered the pearl blinds and wet the silk curtains;
Fur coat couldn't defeat cold and cotton quilt was flimsy;
Bows became rigid, could hardly be drawn
And the congealed metal armor was hard to wear;
The sand-sea deepened with fathomless ice,
And darkness massed its endless clouds;
We drunk to our guest return home from camp,
And played him fiddle, lute, and flutes;
Till at dusk, when the drifts were crushing our tents,

思是：寒冷的北风席卷大地，大风雪压弯了小草，塞北的八月就漫天飘雪。昨晚忽然吹来春风，成千上万的梨树都被包裹成了白色，那洁白的雪花仿佛梨花满树都是。雪花飘散进入珠帘，沾湿了罗幕，穿上狐裘也并不觉得温暖，织锦做成的被子也觉得单薄。就连将军和都护都拉不开弓，他们都觉得盔甲太寒冷，难以穿上。广阔的大漠上百丈

And our frozen red flags could not flutter in the wind,
We saw you off at the east gate of Wheel-tower,
Into the snow covered road of Mount Tianshan.
Till you disappeared at the turn of the mountain pass,
Leaving behind only the hoof-prints on the snowfield.

This is one of the few frontier fortress poems that have magnificent and romantic colors and a fabulous air. It can be regarded as the unsurpassed piece of frontier fortress poetry in the heyday of the Tang Dynasty.

General idea: The chilly west wind blew across the land and tore the grass down. It started to snow heavily early in the eighth-month. Thousands of pear-trees were covered with a layer of white snow like blossoms attached everywhere to the trees, as if a spring gaze just came overnight. The snowflakes flied through pearl blinds, and wet the silk curtains. Even a fur coat didn't feel warm and even a cotton mat seemed thin. What was worse, the bows became rigid, and no one could draw them open, and the metal of armor feeled too icy to wear.

• 白釉陶弹琵琶女俑（隋）
White-glazed Clay Statue of a Female Lute-Player (Sui Dynasty, 581-618)

• 白雪皑皑的塞外风光
Snow-covered Land beyond the Great Wall

厚的坚冰纵横交错，愁云灰暗无光，在万里长空凝聚着。在军中主帅所居的营帐里摆设酒宴，给回去的客人饯行，酒宴上胡琴琵琶与羌笛奏出了热烈欢快的乐曲。傍晚纷纷大雪飘落在辕门外，军旗被冻得很硬，强劲的北风也不能让它飘动。（我）在轮台东门外送你离去，大雪铺满了天山的道路。山路崎岖蜿蜒，不一会儿就看不见你离去的身影，只留下雪地上马走过的蹄印。

Down on the vast sand-sea, fathomless ice lay firm and crisscrossed. Up in the dim sky, clouds of sorrow were grey and dense, gaining strength. Inside the camp, we were giving a farewell dinner to the guest who was leaving soon. We played *huqin* (a Chinese bowed string instrument), lutes, and flutes, whose melodies were merry and cheerful. At dust, the snow was pouring outside the tents, and the red flags were frozen and would not flutter, not even in the violent north wind. We saw the guest off at the east gate of Wheel-tower, while the road of the Mount Tianshan was covered with snow. The road was winding and he soon disappeared, leaving behind only the hoof-prints.

> # 唐诗的诗派

唐诗尽管内容丰富、题材广泛，又有不同的形式和风格，但因为某些具有相似出身、经历或者共同爱好及理想的诗人创作出了具有

· 彩色釉陶骑马男俑（唐）
Multi-color Glazed Clay Statue of a Horse-riding Man (Tang Dynasty, 618-907)

> # Schools of Tang Poetry

Tang poetry, though rich in content and themes and diversified in forms and styles, can be classified into several categories, for certain groups of poets shared similar family background, experience, hobbies and ideals, resulting in poems with similar style and form. Poets in a same category might be intimate friends and was involved in the same political or social circle, thus forming certain schools or groups, consciously or unconsciously. Or, they might be put together and classified into certain schools or groups by scholars in later generations when similarities among those poets as well as their poems were discovered.

Roughly, Tang poetry can be sorted into two main schools: romanticism and realism. Because Chinese literature had

- 《簪花仕女图》周昉（唐）
Court Maids with Head-pinned Flowers, by Zhou Fang (Tang Dynasty, 618-907)

相似风格或形式的作品。这些诗人可能是知己好友，又生活在同一个社会政治圈子中，自觉或不自觉地组成特定的诗派或者团体；又或者是后人在总结唐诗的过程中，发现相似类型的诗人或作品，而将其放在一起，统称为某一派别或团体。

唐诗主要可分为浪漫主义和现实主义两大派别。由于几千年来，中国文学普遍提倡厚重深沉为社会主流，故浪漫主义的诗人和作品在数量和质量上一直处于相对弱势的地位。而在文化相对自由开放的唐朝，浪漫主义诗歌的艺术水平却毫不逊色，迅速发展到高潮，并且先后出现了成就斐然的浪漫主义诗人代表李白、李商隐。现实主义诗歌

called for seriousness and solemnity as its mainstream, romantic poets and poems had been inferior both in quantity and quality. However, in the Tang Dynasty when free and open culture was allowed, the artistic level of romantic poetry was no lower than realistic poetry. It soon reached its peak. The world-famous accomplished romantic poets like Li Bai and Li Shangyin were born and lived in that period. On the realism side is the exemplary Du Fu, who is a representative of realistic poetry, and who has influenced generation after generation since then.

Romantic School

Representative Poet: Li Bai

Characteristics: Romantic poetry

则出现了影响后世颇深的榜样人物杜甫,他开创了现实主义诗歌创作的一代之风。

浪漫主义诗派

代表人物:李白

特点:重视人本身心灵的真实呈现,抒发内心的思想和情感,咏唱对自由、对理想、对个人价值的渴望与追求。用词自由、想象力丰富、思绪天马行空、气势恢宏。诗歌语言清新自然,不事人工雕琢。

代表作:《月下独酌》《梦游天姥吟留别》《蜀道难》等。

现实主义诗派

代表人物:杜甫

特点:现实主义诗歌的艺术风格厚重深沉,贴近现实,兼具思想性、社会性等特质;语言精于雕琢,用词深邃,谋求社会意义和内涵思想的表达;针对现实作出反应,多表现出针砭时弊、悲天悯人的思想和情怀。杜甫诗作是唐朝现实主义诗派作品的代表,他的诗歌在用词、内涵、形式等方面都被后人继承并且发扬光大。从中唐时期

emphasizes faithful presentation of the soul and expression of inner ideas and feelings, by chanting the longing and aspiration for freedom, ideals, and individual values. The wording is unrestrained, and together with wide imaginations, creating an unconstrained, vigorous and powerful effect. This school opposes artificial wording and proposes fresh and natural language.

Master Works: *On Drinking Alone by Moonlight* (*Yuexia Duzhuo*), *Tianmu Mountain Ascended in a Dream* (*Mengyou Tianmu Yin Liubie*), *Hard Roads in Shu* (*Shudao Nan*), etc.

Realistic School

Representative Poet: Du Fu

Characteristics: Realistic poems are serious and solemn in style. They are rooted in reality, combining in a poem ideology and social natures. Poets would work carefully on the language itself and choose profound expressions to deeply interpret social meanings and sophisticated thoughts. They often respond to reality, criticizing social flaws, bewailing the times and pitying the people. Du Fu's poems are the representatives of realistic poetry in the Tang Dynasty. The wording, connotation and narrative pattern of his poems are

到宋代的很多诗人都继承了杜甫的写实风格。

代表作："三吏""三别"及《兵车行》等。

山水田园诗派

代表人物：王维、孟浩然

特点：正如同诗派的名字一样，山水田园诗人们创作的诗歌主要以山水田园等题材为描绘对象。许多唐朝诗人的作品中都会描写自然景物，不过多是为了抒情而借用该物作为铺垫，并不倾注太多笔墨和感情于山水自然本身。而山水田园派诗人则将关注的焦点放在青山白云、绿树田园、溪流湖泊所组合而成的自然风景上，将一种幽人隐士与自然合为一体的淡泊心境融合在风景之中。其诗歌营造出恬静清雅的氛围，富于恬淡之美，将大自然之美全记录在诗中，让后世人也可以从中知道中国几千年以前的风土人情、地理风貌。

代表作：王维的《山居秋暝》《送元二使安西》《九月九日忆山东兄弟》，孟浩然的《过故人庄》。

all inherited and developed by later generations. Many poets from the Mid-Tang period to the Song Dynasty carried on Du Fu's realistic style.

Master Works: "The Sergeant Trilogy" (*Sanli*, three serial poems about sergeant), "The Parting Trilogy" (*Sanbie*, three serial poems about separation), *Song of the Conscripts* (*Bingche Xing*), etc.

Landscape and Pastoral Poetic School

Representative Poets: Wang Wei, Meng Haoran

Characteristics: Just as its name implied, verses written by landscape and pastoral poets mainly took landscapes, pastoral scenes and other themes as the delineative objects. In many poems written by poets of the Tang Dynasty, natural scenes were portrayed, while most of them were borrowed to pave the way for expressing the poets' emotions. The poets did not pour too many words and feelings into nature itself. However, these poets concentrated on the landscapes composed by green hills and white cloud, greenery and countryside, streams and lakes, they integrated a simple state of mind, which united seclusion and nature as one into landscapes. The quiet and light atmosphere the poems made was full of beauty of indifference to fame. The beauty of nature was also recorded in the poems, from which the later generations can take a glimpse on China's local conditions and customs as well as geographical features thousands of years ago.

Master Works: *Autumn Evening in the Mountains* (*Shanju Qiuming*), *Seeing Yuan Er Off to Anxi* (*Song Yuan Er Shi Anxi*), *Remembering the Brothers in Shandong on September 9th of Lunar Calendar* (*Jiuyue Jiuri Yi Shandong Xiongdi*), by Wang Wei; *Passing the Village of Old Friends* (*Guo Guren Zhuang*), by Meng Haoran.

Frontier Fortress Poetic School

Representative Poets: Wang Changling, Cen Shen

Characteristics: The birth of this school had close relation to the state condition of the Tang Dynasty. Because the battles broke out frequently in the border area, many poets experienced relegation and relocation or they volunteered for military service. Naturally, their poems were based on

• 《桃源仙境图》仇英（明）
The Fairy Land of Peach Blossoms, by Qiu Ying (Ming Dynasty, 1368-1644)

边塞诗派

代表人物：王昌龄、岑参

特点：边塞诗派的产生和唐朝的国情紧密相关，唐朝边境地区战事频繁，许多诗人都有或贬谪、调职，或主动请缨去边境地区参军服役的生活经历。其创作也自然以他们亲身所见、所闻、所感为基础，边塞诗由此产生。诗歌主要描写的是战争的残酷，战场的辽阔，还有寒冷苍茫的大漠风景以及离家万里驻守边关壮烈牺牲的将士们。在豪迈悲壮的诗句中，诗人称颂的是将士们的英勇精神，描绘的是边塞风光的雄浑壮美和奇异的风土人情，揭露的是战争的残酷、惨烈及驻守边关的孤独和艰辛，表达的是向往和平、稳定、和睦的情怀。

代表作：王昌龄《出塞》、岑参《白雪歌送武判官归京》等。

their own findings, hearings or feelings, and for this the frontier poetry appeared. The major coverage of the poems were the cruelty of war, the extensiveness of battlefield, cold and boundless desert landscape as well as soldiers who defended the frontier junctures that were far away from their homes, and sacrificed their lives. By using the solemn and stirring verses, poets praised the heroic spirit of the soldiers, portrayed the magnificence and beauty of frontier fortress scenery and fantastic customs, disclosed the cruelty and terribleness of war as well as the solitude and hardships of defending the frontier and expressed the feelings of yearning for peace, stability and harmoniousness.

Master Works: *On the Frontier (Chusai)*, by Wang Changling; *Seeing Assistant Wu Back to Chang'an in the Snow (Baixue Ge Song Wu Panguan Guijing)*, by Cen Shen.

• 《牧马图》韩幹（唐）
Herding Horses, by Han Gan (Tang Dynasty, 618-907)

大历十才子

"大历"是唐代宗的年号,"十才子"就是当时诗坛比较有名且具有相似特点的十位诗人,他们分别是李端、卢纶、吉中孚、韩翃、钱起、司空曙、苗发、崔峒、耿湋、夏侯审。"大历十才子"所代表的是一个专有的诗歌流派,形成于唐诗由盛唐向中唐过渡的时期。大历诗人们正是经历了"安史之乱"后,唐朝逐渐由强盛转入衰落的历史时期。他们创作的诗中很难再出现盛唐的自信和气

Ten Talents in Dali Period

"Dali" was the reign title of Emperor Li Yu of the Tang Dynasty; "Ten Talents" were ten outstanding poets who shared similar characteristics at that time, including Li Duan, Lu Lun, Ji Zhongfu, Han Hong, Qian Qi, Sikong Shu, Miao Fa, Cui Tong, Geng Wei, Xiahou Shen. What "Ten Talents in Dali Period" represented was a specialized poetic school, which was formed in a transient period from the blooming to the middle stage of the Tang Dynasty. These poets lived in a historical period when the Tang Dynasty gradually fell into a decline after An-Shi Rebellion (755-763). It is difficult to see the self-confidence and boldness of the blooming Tang, as well as the wrath and solemnness towards the wars in their poems. As the fact of the sudden decline of the Tang Dynasty, their works showed lonely and weak and the style turned from forceful to peaceful. Therefore, "Ten Talents in Dali Period", though became a poetic school as their special references of that time, it didn't praised highly by the later generations or make outstanding

- 《双骑图》韦偃(唐)
  Duet Riding, Wei Yan (Tang Dynasty, 618-907)

魄，也没有经历苦难战争的激愤和悲壮。如同中唐在由巅峰突然下滑到低谷的无奈现实一样，大历诗人的作品显得落寞柔弱，风格由雄浑转向淡远。因此在诗坛上，"大历十才子"虽然因为具有中唐的时代气息而成为一种诗派，但并不为后人所推崇，诗歌成就也并不算出众，很快就被重新振作的诗坛新人所取代。

代表作：李端《听筝》、卢纶《塞下曲四首》

韩孟诗派

"韩孟诗派"的"韩"是指韩愈（768—824），"孟"是指孟郊（751—814）。韩孟诗派是中唐时期由一群志同道合的诗人自发形成的诗歌创作流派。这个诗人团体以韩愈为代表，包括孟郊、李贺等许多中唐时期有名气的诗人。他们都主张"不平则鸣"，写诗就要抒发内心的感情，崇尚奇险怪异，追求光怪陆离、五彩斑斓的艺术境界。诗人们互相切磋酬唱，提倡他们与众不同、诡异奇特的审美趣味。韩孟诗派的诗人们在创作时有意打破诗歌传统的表现手法，故意使用艰

achievement, and was gradually replaced by the revived new poets.

Master Works: *Listening to the Chinese Zither* (*Ting Zheng*), by Li Duan; *Four Frontier Songs* (*Saixia Qu Sishou*), by Lu Lun.

Han-Meng Poetic School

"Han-Meng poetic school", "Han" indicating Han Yu (768-824), "Meng" indicating Meng Jiao (751-814), which was a poetic school formed spontaneously by a group of poets who had a common goal in the middle Tang Dynasty. With Han Yu as its representative, this group had many well-known poets such as Meng Jiao and Li He. They stood for the philosophy of "injustice provoking outcry", meaning writing poems is to express the emotions; and pursued the strange, bizarre and colorful aesthetic taste. Through consulting each poem, these poets learnt from each other, they also advocated an aesthetic taste out of the ordinary and commonplace. In poetry creation, they broke the traditional technique of expression on purpose and used abstract words to change the fixed requirement of rules and forms of classical poems. With images

● **韩愈像**

韩愈（768—824），字退之，唐代古文运动的倡导者，明人推他为唐宋八大家之首，有"文章巨公"和"百代文宗"之名。他的诗歌风格恣肆横放、雄奇险怪，常常运用奇特想象和夸张变形的手法，创造出奇异怪诞的意象。

Portrait of Han Yu

Han Yu (768-824), courtesy name *Tuizhi*, was an initiator of Ancient Literature Movement in the Tang Dynasty. People in the Ming Dynasty respected him as the head of "Eight Prose Masters of the Tang-Song Period" and he was also called "Literary Giant" or "Eternal Model of Literati". With an unrestrained, imposing and strange style, his poems often created strange images by peculiar imagination and exaggeration and metabolic technique of writing.

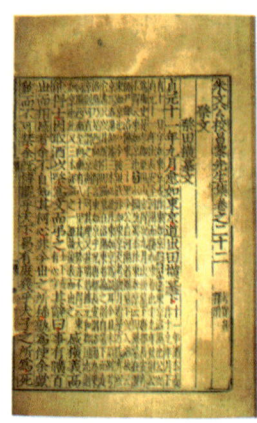

● **元刻本《朱文公校昌黎先生集》**

韩愈郡望昌黎（今辽宁义县），所以又称韩昌黎。《昌黎先生集》是韩愈的诗文作品集，共十卷。朱文公，指南宋儒学大家朱熹。

Block-printed Edition of *Mr. Changli's Collection*, *Proofread by Zhu Wengong* (Yuan Dynasty, 1206-1368)

Han Yu's ancestral home was Changli (present Yi County in Liaoning Province), so he was also called Han Changli. *Mr. Changli's Collection* was his collected works of poems and prose, with 10 volumes in total. Zhu Wengong indicates Zhu Xi, authority of Confucianism in the Southern Song Dynasty (1127-1279).

深的字词，改变格律的固定要求。描写的诗歌意象怪奇险峻，构思奇特，形成一种奇险俊逸的艺术审美风格，在当时的诗坛算得上是标新立异，一改大历诗风的平弱纤巧。韩孟诗派追求诗歌创作改革创新的行为，直接导致唐诗的创作风格、题材和作者都发生了新的变化，积

bewildering and precipitous, conception being discursive, their poems formed a strange but majestic aesthetic style, which were unique and unprecedented in the Parnassus that time and changed the weak and dainty style in Dali period. The reform and innovation that Han-Meng poetic school launched led to the new changes of Tang poetry in creative

极推动了盛唐以后诗人们对诗歌艺术创作领域的开拓。

代表作：韩愈《南山诗》《调张籍》《山石》，孟郊《秋怀十五首》《答友人赠炭》。

元白诗派

元白诗派和韩孟诗派一样，也是以诗人为核心而形成的诗歌流派。"元"就是元稹（779—831），"白"就是白居易。元白诗派以他们二人为代表，出现的时间与韩孟诗派相近，但艺术风格却与韩孟诗派截然不同。韩孟诗派追求新奇，而元白诗派恰恰相反。他们注重写实，推崇通俗，使用简单明了的语言来创作，力求接近现实生活和大众审美。白居易是中国古代少数几个用白话来写诗的诗人，诗歌语言通俗易懂，内容贴近人们的生活，便于吟咏和记忆，所以他的诗流传很广。元白诗派在诗歌的通俗化发展方面作出了许多努力。元白发起的新乐府运动，强调诗歌惩恶扬善、补察时政的功能，提倡通俗易解的诗歌语言，从另一个方面丰富拓宽了唐诗创作的领域，和韩

style, theme and writers and promoted the development of artistic creation field after the blooming Tang.

Master Works: *South Hill Poetry* (*Nanshan Shi*), *Joking with Zhang Ji*, *Mountain Stones* (*Shanshi*), by Han Yu; *Fifteen Verses of Autumn Feelings* (*Qiuhuai Shiwushou*), *Answer to the Charcoal Presentation From My Friend* (*Da Youren Zengtan*), by Meng Jiao.

Yuan-Bai Poetic School

Same as "Han-Meng poetic school", "Yuan-Bai poetic school" was also a poetic school formed on the basis of poets: "Yuan" indicating Yuan Zhen (779-831) and "Bai" indicating Bai Juyi (772-846). Represented by them two, Yuan-Bai Poetic School appeared almost at the same time with Han-Meng poetic school, while they had entirely different artistic style. Han-Meng poetic school sought for novelty, on the contrary, Yuan-Bai poetic school paid attention to realistic writing and held popularity in esteem. They wrote poems by simple and clear words and tried to come close to real life and catered for mass aesthetics. Bai Juyi was one of few poets who wrote poems in colloquial language in ancient China. With the

孟诗派一起为唐诗的发展做出了杰出的贡献。

代表作：白居易《长恨歌》、元稹《连昌宫词》。

language easily understood and contents closed to people's life, his poems were easy to chant and memorize. That's why his works were handed down so widely. Yuan-Bai poetic school made great endeavor in the popularization of poetry and initiated the New Ballads (*Yuefu*) Movement, which emphasized the function of poems in punishing evil-doers and praising good-doers as well as making amends for current political mistakes, advocated the legibility of poetry and expanded the creation realm of the poetry-writing on the other hand. Together with Han-Meng poetic school, it made great contribution to the development of Tang poetry.

Master Works: *Song of Eternal Sorrow* (*Changhen Ge*), by Bai Juyi; *Lianchang Palace Poem* (*Lianchang Gong Ci*), by Yuan Zhen.

● **元稹像**

元稹，字微之，唐洛阳（今河南洛阳）人。其诗歌风格于平浅明快中呈现华美，色彩浓烈，铺叙曲折，细节刻画真切动人。他曾留下悼念亡妻的千古名句："曾经沧海难为水，除却巫山不是云。"

Portrait of Yuan Zhen

Yuan Zhen, courtesy name Weizhi, was a native of Luoyang (present Luoyang City in Henan Province). With evident feature, circuitous narration, realistic and moving detail depiction, his poems presented magnificence in a lucid and lively style. He left a famous verse in memory of his dead wife: "No water's enough when you have crossed the sea; No cloud is beautiful but that floating above Mount Wu".

著名诗人与唐诗作品
Famous Poets and Works

  唐朝诗人耀如繁星，所创作的著名诗篇脍炙人口、流传千古。诗人们风格各异，百花齐放，百家争鸣。他们的诗歌诉尽天上人间事，悲欢离合情；他们的诗中有天才的惊世骇俗，也有勤奋的笔耕不辍，有惊天地泣鬼神的悲天悯人，也有淡然幽静的山水田园，还有辽阔壮观的边塞豪情。本部分将呈现著名唐诗作品和诗人的传奇经历。

Like stars in the sky, poets in the Tang Dynasty were both brilliant and numerous. Famous poems created by them enjoyed great popularity and good fame throughout ages. With various styles and diversified forms, they told stories in the world, expressed joys, sorrows, partings and reunions in poetry. Some were genius who shocked the society; some were diligent men who never gave up writing; some expressed compassion for the state of the world and its people; some described the quiet landscapes; some expressed the lofty sentiments at the extensive frontier fortress; etc. In this part, the fascinating poems and the legendary experiences of poets will be told in a pleasing way.

> "诗仙"李白

李白（701—762），字太白，号青莲居士，中国历史上少有的天才诗人，他在诗歌创作上的惊人才华和鲜明风格令人赞叹。他打破当时封建正统思想对人心灵的束缚，恣意发挥个人的想象力、创造力，在唐诗各种体裁的创作中达到近乎完美的境界。他的诗歌，意境瑰丽神奇，语言清新自然，妙句巧夺天工，充满引人入胜的艺术魅力。李白崇尚自由，自信洒脱，狂放不羁，既是一个傲视一切、恃才放旷的浪漫主义诗人，又是一个胸怀大志、特立独行的侠士。他的名字在中国家喻户晓，甚至被当成唐诗的代言。唐朝的著名诗人数不胜数，犹如满天星辰，而李白就是其中最

> "Poetry Immortal" Li Bai

Li Bai (701-762), courtesy name Taibai and self-titled Qinglian Jushi (meaning householder of the Azure Lotus), was a genius scarcely seen in Chinese history. His brilliant talent in poetry creation and bright style won him high praise. He broke up the bonds of feudal orthodoxy on people's spirit, exerted personal imaginations and creativity at his will and reached an almost perfect situation in various genres of Tang poetry creation. Poems written by him, which had miraculous artistic conception, pure and fresh language and wonderful phrase, were full of fascinating artistic charm. Striving for liberty and leading an unconventional life, Li Bai was a self-confident and big-hearted man, not only a romantic poet who was arrogant and

• 《太白醉酒图》苏六朋（清）
Drunken Taibai, by Su Liupeng (Qing Dynasty, 1616-1911)

为耀眼的一颗。

　　李白从小就受到良好的文学熏陶，并且精通剑术，可谓文武全才。他成长在巴蜀地区，那里崇

unconstrained of his ability, but also a swordsman who aimed high and acted independently. With his name widely known in China, he was even considered as the prolocutor of Tang poetry. Just as stars in the sky, famous poets in Tang Dynasty were innumerous, while Li Bai was the most brilliant one.

　　When he was a child, Li Bai had a good nurture of literature. Moreover, he mastered swordsmanship. It may be said that he was a man of both literary and military talents. He grew up in Ba-Shu area, which has full of lofty mountains, curled clouds, interlaced hills and waters, and unique and beautiful landscapes, making it a fairy land for many lofty hermits to seclude. There is an idiom in China "*Diling Renjie*", which means a remarkable place produces outstanding people. Li Bai was a genius of literature who went out from this "fairyland". Being arrogant for his talent, Li Bai was unwilling to become an official through civil servant examination. Instead, he relied on his talents and hoped to reach the high power and realize his political ideals through recommendation. In his twenties, Li Bai left Ba-Shu area and began his days of wandering. He made friends and visited socialites. More than

● 根雕李白像（现代）
Root Carving Statue of Li Bai (Modern Times)

山峻岭、云烟缭绕、山水相间，独特秀丽的风景仿若仙境，是许多世外高人隐居的地方。中国有句成语叫"地灵人杰"，意思是山川秀丽的地方有灵气，会熏陶培养出杰出的人才。李白就是在这片"仙境"里走出来的文学奇才。李白恃才傲物，不愿通过应试科举的途径做官，而是希望依靠自身才华，通过他人举荐一举登上高位，去实现政治理想和抱负。他二十岁时离开巴蜀，开始了广泛的漫游。他结交朋友，拜谒社会名流，可是十几年漫游，却一事无成。直到天宝元年

ten years had passed by, but he achieved nothing. Until the first year of Period Tianbao (742), Li Bai finally got the recommendation, which led Emperor Li Longji to summon him to the court in Chang'an. He got a post at the Hanlin Academy, where his poems shocked the whole China. However, his undisciplined and prideful individuality brought him envy and hate of influential officials. Only three years later, he gave up his post and continued his wandering. In An-Shi Rebellion (755-763), he served for the office of Prince Yong, who later made his bid for the imperial power with Emperor Li Heng but failed. Upon the defeat of the Prince's forces, Li Bai was captured and later exiled. He was subsequently pardoned before he ever reached the destination. Li didn't cease his wandering lifestyle in his later years and eventually, he died of illness in Dangtu county, Anhui Province.

Li Bai's poems were full of gorgeous imaginations, which were expressed fully by wonderful verses: "Yellow River's waters running from the heaven" described the tremendous momentum of the forceful Yellow River's waters that poured into sea from unmeasured sky; by using an extremely exaggeration

（742），李白终于得到举荐，被唐玄宗召至长安，供奉翰林，文章风采，名震天下。然而李白狂放自傲的个性，被权贵们所嫉恨，在京仅三年就弃官而去，仍然继续他飘荡四方的游历生活。在"安史之乱"中，他曾投身永王的幕府效力，但后来永王与唐肃宗争夺皇帝之位，兵败之后，李白也被连累流放，途中遇赦。他晚年继续漂泊，最后病逝于安徽当涂县。

李白的诗歌充满了绮丽跳跃的想象力，他运用巧夺天工的诗句将这种奇特想象淋漓尽致地表达出来。"黄河之水天上来"描绘出雄浑的黄河水从广阔无垠的高空中倾泻而下、直冲入海时的磅礴气势；"白发三千丈"用极其夸张、完全不合常理的长度单位形容白发，表达惆怅的程度；"抽刀断水水更流"，用常人不会想到的举刀来砍断流水的意象来比喻排解忧愁。即使明知水流一如既往地流动根本不会断，但是，这种因内心的无比惆怅而采用的一种悲壮激昂的方式，不仅没有令人暗自幽怨，反而倍感振奋的气势。这些都是只有李白才能够创造出来的句子。与其他诗人

and totally unreasonable length unit to describe his white hair, "My white hair is three thousand *Zhang* (a unit of length, equals to 3 and 1/3 meters) long" expressed the poet's melancholy; "Cut running water with a sword will only quicken the flow", to escape from sadness, the poet cut the flowing water by his sword, even he knew that the flowing water could not be cut, which was a method that out of ordinary people's imagination. However, this solemn and stirring method of expressing the unbelievable melancholy did not make people feel sad, instead, it expressed an exhilarated momentum. These verses could only be created by Li Bai. Compared with other poets, his biggest characteristic was unconstrained and unconventional. Getting rid of the rules and conventions that were obeyed by ordinary people, Li Bai's poems took on an elegant style: natural, unconventional and idealist, so later generations addressed him respectfully as "Poetry Immortal".

As a poem written by Li Bai, *Bringing in the Wine* was not only his portrayal of attitude towards life, but also a reflection of his heroic and generous character. That was the reason why his

相比，他最大的特点就是无拘无束、独立不羁。因为摆脱了凡夫俗子们的循规蹈矩、迂腐守旧，展现出自然超脱和理想主义的飘逸风格，所以后世尊称李白为"诗仙"。

　　李白的《将进酒》不仅是他的人生态度的写照，也是他豪迈慷慨性格的体现，这正是他的诗风不同凡响、气壮如山的原因之所在。

将进酒

君不见黄河之水天上来，
奔流到海不复回。
君不见高堂明镜悲白发，
朝如青丝暮成雪。
人生得意须尽欢，莫使金樽空对月。
天生我材必有用，千金散尽还复来。
烹羊宰牛且为乐，会须一饮三百杯。
岑夫子，丹丘生，将进酒，杯莫停。
与君歌一曲，请君为我倾耳听。
钟鼓馔玉不足贵，但愿长醉不复醒。
古来圣贤皆寂寞，惟有饮者留其名。
陈王昔时宴平乐，斗酒十千恣欢谑。
主人何为言少钱，径须沽取对君酌。
五花马，千金裘，呼儿将出换美酒，
与尔同销万古愁。

poetic style was so outstanding and inspiring.

Bringing In the Wine

See how the Yellow River's waters running from the heaven.
Entering the ocean, never to return.
See how the people feeling sad on their white hair in the hall,
Though silken-black at morning, have changed by night to snow.
Let a man of spirit venture where he pleases,
And never tip his golden cup empty toward the moon.
Since God gave the talent, let it be employed!
Spend out a thousand pieces of silver which will come back someday.
Cook a lamb, kill a cattle, whet the appetite,
And make me, of three hundred bowls, one long drink.
To the old master, Cen, and the young scholar, Danqiu,
Bringing in the wine, Let your cups never rest.
Let me sing you a song,
Let your ears attend!
Rare dishes and treasure are not precious at all,
Let me be forever drunk and never come to reason!
Sober men of olden days and sages were all alone,

开头两句，李白从空间和时间的角度来慨叹时间如梭，生命飞逝，开篇宏伟，先声夺人，从一开始就给人营造一种开阔发散的想象空间，让人充分理解他的诗歌意境。后世虽也有诗人的开篇能有此水准，但却难以达到《将进酒》整篇雄浑、挥洒自如的境界。

李白人生中最辉煌的岁月就是作为御用文人侍奉唐玄宗的三年，但他特立独行、与众不同的为人处世风格招来了嫉恨。传说有一天，皇帝传召李白进宫写诗，他当时已在酒肆烂醉如泥。被抬进宫后，唐玄宗让著名宦官高力士给李白脱去靴子让他舒服一些，李白竟然毫

• 李白脱靴
Taking off Boots for Li Bai

And only the great drinkers were famous in history.
Prince Chen paid at a banquet in the Palace of Perfection,
Ten thousand coins for a cask of wine, with many a laugh and quip.
Why say, my host, that your money is gone,
Go and buy wine and we'll drink it together.
My flower-dappled horse, my furs worth a thousand,
Hand them to the boy to exchange for good wine,
And we'll drown away the woes of ten thousand generations.

In the first two sentences, Li Bai heaves a sigh about the time that has passed by from the perspectives of space and time. At the very beginning, it gives people enough space for imagination so that people can understand the artistic conception of the poem. The later generations of poets can hardly match Li Bai in terms of the grace and ease of the poem, though they might match him in the beginning of the poem.

The best years of Li Bai's life were spent serving as a hired scribbler for Emperor Li Longji, until he caused grudge because of his different way and attitude of life. Legend has it that

不客气欣然接受。按照唐朝的等级制度，高力士当时是地位显赫的官员，而李白只是一个下级小吏，怎么能让地位更高的官员为自己脱鞋呢？这是极为不敬的。高力士由此生出怨恨，后来阴谋陷害了李白，令他被皇帝放逐。虽然这个传说不一定属实，但李白后来不得不离开朝廷，的确是因为他的清高个性造成的。即便他的人生因此进入低谷期，为无法实现"兼济天下"的人生抱负而满腹忧愁，但仍不改豁达狂放的个性，所以接下来的诗句"人生得意须尽欢，莫使金樽空对

one day Li Bai was called into court to write poems, but he was as drunk as a fiddler, so when Emperor Li Longji had the eunuch Gao Lishi took off Li Bai's boots, Li Bai's did not refuse, which caused Gao's hatred because Gao was of high social status at that time and Li Bai should have refused according to the then convention. Later, Li Bai was set up by Gao and was exiled to distant land. The legend might not be true, but Li Bai did have to leave the court, which was viewed as a result of his arrogant personality. After that, Li Bai's life entered a miserable stage and he was filled with sorrow and anxiety because his ambition "well-being under heaven" could not be achieved. But his arrogant personality remained unchanged, which could be seen in his later poem to encourage himself "Let a man of spirit venture where he pleases, and never tip his golden cup empty toward the moon. Since God gave the talent, let it be employed! Spend out a thousand pieces of silver which will come back someday." Numerous later people like Li Bai would recite this poem to reassure themselves when they were in failure, frustration and despair. Li Bai's confidence and composure about his talent made him

● 翡翠雕刻摆件《太白醉酒》
Emerald Carving Ornament with the Theme of *Drunken Taibai*

《藏云图》【局部】崔子忠（明）

此图取材于李白的故事。相传李白居地肺山时，曾以瓶甑贮存山中的浓云带回居所，散之卧内，得以"日饮清泉卧白云"。

Hidden Cloud (Part), by Cui Zizhong (Ming Dynasty, 1368-1644)

This picture is originated from tales of Li Bai. According to the folk story, Li Bai ever used a bottle to store the mountain's thick cloud and took it back home, so that he could "drink clean spring and lie on the white cloud every day" after he spread out the cloud in his bedroom.

月。天生我材必有用，千金散尽还复来"正是他勉励自己的话。后世有多少人在失败、沮丧、落魄时，都会吟咏这豪迈潇洒的千古名句来自我开解，求得安慰。李白对自身

optimistic in front of injustices of life and never cease to enjoy life. Such state of mind was very rare in the then society led by feudal thought and was kind of like immortal.

"Cook a lamb, kill a cattle, whet the appetite, and make me, of three hundred bowls, one long drink. To the old master, Cen, and the young scholar, Danqiu, bringing in the wine, let your cups never rest. Let me sing you a song, let your ears attend! Rare dishes and treasure are not precious at all, let me be forever drunk and never come to reason! Sober men of olden days and sages were all alone, and only the great drinkers were famous in history." These several sentences from the poem was a vivid description of the movie-like scene bustling with noise and excitement when Li Bai was having fun drinking and singing with his friends: With wine pot on one hand and writing brush on the other, Li Bai was shuttling back and forward among his friends and urged them to drink, while at the same time, he sang loudly and then wrote this famous poem at one stretch when he was inspired by his poetic creation. Though it seemed that Li Bai was just talking about drinking, even those who read his poem would know Li Bai's state of mind of

才华能力的自信和笃定，使他豁达乐观地面对人生的种种不平，无论何时都不忘享受生活，及时行乐，这种心态在当时封建思想主导的功利社会中实属罕见，颇有超脱世俗的"仙风道骨"。

"烹羊宰牛且为乐，会须一饮三百杯。岑夫子，丹丘生，将进酒，杯莫停。与君歌一曲，请君为我倾耳听。钟鼓馔玉不足贵，但愿长醉不复醒。古来圣贤皆寂寞，惟有饮者留其名。"这几句诗把李白爱喝酒唱歌，与朋友聚会时的觥筹交错、热闹非凡的场面刻画得形象生动、跃然纸上，仿佛是电影中的一幕：李白一手提着酒壶，一手拿着毛笔，一边在朋友中间穿梭劝酒，一边引吭高歌，一时诗兴大发，在纸上一气呵成写出这首诗。尽管表面上他一直在谈喝酒，但读到这首诗的人都能感觉到李白借酒消愁的心境。

"陈王昔时宴平乐，斗酒十千恣欢谑。主人何为言少钱，径须沽取对君酌。五花马，千金裘，呼儿将出换美酒，与尔同销万古愁。"还是在继续铺陈他的一掷千金换美酒的万丈豪情，直到最后一句才

sorrow and anxiety.

"Prince Chen paid at a banquet in the Palace of Perfection, ten thousand coins for a cask of wine, with many a laugh and quip. Why say, my host, that your money is gone, go and buy wine and we'll drink it together. My flower-dappled horse, my furs worth a thousand. Hand them to the boy to exchange for good wine, and we'll drown away the woes of ten thousand generations." These sentences are just a further description of his bold and unconstrained personality that he would swap lots of money for wine while the last sentence was his real thought:

• 紫砂泥塑《李白醉酒》
Purple Sands Clay Sculpture of *Drunken Li Bai*

终于道出了内心真实的想法：喝酒其实是为了消解这"千万年的深深哀愁"。在看似纵情欢乐的表面之下，其实隐藏着他内心无限的哀愁，这份哀愁甚至有"万古"那么深远，这份深沉的感情成功地为全诗画下了完美的句号。在李白强颜欢笑的背后，是壮志未酬的哀愁与幽怨。借酒消愁是中国千百年来历代文人具有的一种共通的心境，而李白的诗句则将其表达得酣畅淋漓。单从这一首诗里，就能读到李白高超的诗歌技艺、昂扬潇洒的人生态度和壮志难酬的悲壮情怀。

drinking was just his way of dissolving his "woes of ten thousand generation", which could hardly been seen from his seemingly joyful face. The woes are so deep that it served as a perfect stop for the poem. Behind Li Bai's joyful face were his sorrow and bitterness that his ambition could not be achieved. Li Bai's poem was a full and smooth description of drinking wine to dissolve sorrow, a historically common state of mind for scholars in China. Just by reading this single poem, we can see Li Bai's superb poetic skill, graceful life attitude and the sorrows of unaccomplished ambitions.

> "诗圣"杜甫

杜甫（712—770），字子美，自号少陵野老，被后人尊称为"诗圣"，他与好友"诗仙"李白堪称中国文学史上璀璨耀眼的双子星。

> "Poetry Sage" Du Fu

Du Fu (712-770), whose courtesy name was "Zimei" and self-titled name "Shaoling Yelao" (referring to himself, an old man who lived in Shaoling, a town in Xi'an, Shaanxi Province), was later honored as the "Poetry Sage" by the later generations. He and his friend Li Bai who was respected as "Poetry Immortal" can be compared to the most glorious Gemini in the history of Chinese literature. While Li Bai was the leader of the Romantic school, Du Fu could be the uncrowned king of the realist school. Li Bai's poems were full of magnificent and fantastic imagination, ideas and like exploring in the sky freely. Even when he was sad, he could express impassioned,

• 杜甫草堂内的杜甫像
Portrait of Du Fu in His Thatched Cottage

如果说李白是浪漫主义派的领军人物，那么杜甫就是现实主义派的无冕之王。李白的诗歌字里行间充满瑰丽奇幻的想象，天马行空，气势磅礴，即使悲伤也是慷慨激昂、洒脱奔放，很有诗仙风范。而杜甫的诗歌则饱含沉郁忧患，深沉厚重，将人间情态摹写得细密真切，令人动容。他的诗歌大都关注生活的细微点滴，描写当时社会的民生百态，就像是一本记录历史的心情日记，表达担忧国家兴亡、忧患民族危难的思想感情，悲情文字力透纸

free and easy flowing emotions, which show the manner of Poetry Immortal. But Du Fu's poems were more concerned with the gloomy hardship and heavy burdens of life. He described the social realities in detail which made people moved. His worries for the fate and crisis of the nation were expressed in his poems which were like a mood diary recording the history. So the tragic emotions were curved directly to people's hearts by the characters and moved a lot of people. Du Fu's studious diligence paid off. In his middle and later years, he reached

- **杜甫草堂茅屋故居**

杜甫初到成都时，在浣花溪畔空地上盖了一间茅屋，这个新家常常遭受到大风的袭击。一年秋天，大风几乎将屋顶上的茅草吹得一干二净。在著名诗篇《茅屋为秋风所破歌》中，杜甫发出了这样的呼声："安得广厦千万间，大庇天下寒士俱欢颜，风雨不动安如山！"（怎么才能得到千万间宽敞高大的房子，庇覆天下贫寒的读书人，让他们开颜欢笑，房子在风雨中也不为所动，安稳得像山一样。）

Du Fu's Former Residence in His Thatched Cottage

When Du Fu first arrived in Chengdu, he built a thatched cottage on the empty land near Huanhua River. His new home was often subjected to wind attacks. One autumn, the wind almost blew away the roof of the cottage. In the famous poem, *Thatched Hut Wrecked by the Autumn Wind (Maowu Wei Qiufeng Suopo Ge)*, Du Fu cried: "Oh, for a ten thousand great mansions, where all the poor on earth could find warm shelter, steady through every storm and secure as a mountain!" (How can I get ten thousand large and tall houses to shelter the world's poor people and let them be joyful in the house? And how can I keep the houses stable like mountains in the wind and rain?)

背、真挚感人。杜甫好学勤奋，厚积薄发。到中老年的时候，他的创作达到巅峰。如果说李白的才华是浑然天成的，那么杜甫的才华就是精心打磨的，两人的诗歌都达到了令人景仰的极高水平和境界，后人将二人并称为"李杜"。读唐诗必读"李杜"，方能领略唐诗的精华之所在。

杜甫比李白晚出生十几年，经历了导致唐王朝由强大转为衰落的"安史之乱"。当时到处兵荒马乱，战争不断，百姓流离失所、生活困苦不堪。杜甫本人也在战乱

his peak in writing. While Li Bai was born talent, Du Fu's ability was carefully polished and their poems all leveled high, which were respected by descendants who named them as "Li-Du". Their poems are necessary when learning poems in the Tang Dynasty, in reading which can the readers grasp the essence and classics of Tang poems.

Du Fu, who was ten years younger than Li Bai, experienced the An-Shi Rebellion (755-763), the civil war which changed the Tang Dynasty from thrive to decline. At that time, chaos of continued wars were everywhere and people were displaced and lived in squalor. Du Fu himself, also experiencing a variety of hardships in the war, survived after fleeing to different places. The bitter reality changed his sensitivity into inner melancholy. He had always most admired the prime minister of Kingdom of Shu-Han (221-263) Zhuge Liang who served his country and people wholeheartedly to the end of his life. Du hoped to serve the country, defend and benefit the common people like Zhuge Liang. He even risked his life to go alone to the place where the emperor was besieged by the enemy to defend him. This dauntless spirit of sacrifice at the time was very

• 木雕杜甫像
Wood Carving Statue of Du Fu

中经历了各种磨难，四处逃亡，死里逃生。这种苦难的现实让本来就内心敏感的他更加忧郁。他一向最崇拜为国为民"鞠躬尽瘁，死而后已"的蜀汉丞相诸葛亮，一直希望像诸葛亮一样为国效力、拯救苍生、造福黎民，甚至还曾冒着生命危险只身前往皇帝被敌军围困的地方忠诚护主。这种大无畏的牺牲精神在当时是非常值得称道的。然而他的忠心和才能并没有得到皇帝的赏识，和许多唐朝诗人才子的命运一样，杜甫一生未得重用，始终郁郁不得志。

任凭风雨飘摇，杜甫的报国之心矢志不渝。即使身处贫穷和痛苦的困境之中，他也始终心系国家和百姓的安危。他逃亡到边境时，发现可能会对唐王朝不利的边境军事异动，就在诗歌中记录下来以示警醒；看见百姓生活艰难，为兵役、赋税所累，苦不堪言，他就在诗中叙述实情，揭露统治的弊端；听说唐王朝的军队打了胜仗收复了失地，就在诗歌中表达喜悦之情、激动不已；得知一位忠诚的将军被诬陷夺去兵权，他就在诗中大声疾

commendable. However, his loyalty and talent weren't appreciated by the emperor, and he was frustrated like many poets in the Tang Dynasty with the ignorance of the imperial court.

Despite the precarious situations, Du Fu's serving the country was determined. Even living in the plight of poverty and suffering, he was always mindful of the country and people's safety. When he fled to the border and found the unusual military actions that might pose a threat to the Tang court, he would record them in poems to show alert; when perceiving people's difficulties caused by military service and taxes, he would describe the truth in his poems and reveal the shortcomings of the rule; after hearing of the victory of Tang's army and the regain of lost lands, he was very joyous and excited which were also expressed in his poems; when knowing that a loyal general was deprived of his power by a false charge, he would repine at his experience in his poems. Though neither these poems nor his sincere heart might be known by the emperor, Du Fu never thought of changing his loyalty to the emperor and his aspiration to save the world till the last moment of life. The noble sentiments of love was admired by

呼为其鸣不平……尽管这些诗作未必被皇帝所知，尽管一片赤诚并不被皇帝所识，但直到生命的最后一刻，杜甫对国家对人民的一片真情未改，想要拯救苍生的心愿未变。这种大爱的高尚情操为后人所敬仰，所以人们在称赞杜甫诗作的同时，更加推崇他忧国忧民的"圣人"般高尚的品格。

杜甫将所见所闻所经历的政治、历史、生活中的各个方面都用诗歌记录下来，并且尽量从客观的角度去观察事物本身，他在完成诗歌的同时，也是一种对历史的记录，所以他的诗又被称为"诗史"。

the later generations, so people praised the poems of Du Fu and respected his lofty spirit which were also shown by the name "Sage".

Du Fu described all aspects of his experiences in politics, history and life and tried to observe from an objective point of the thing itself. At the time when he completed his poems he also recorded history, and therefore, his poems were also called "Poetry History".

Du Fu's best and most successful poems were the *Lvshi* (a poem of eight lines). Before him, most of this kind was tailored as gifts, while Du's were written to reflect wider social life. Due to the strict metrical writing verses, poets would either fall into the vulgar ones, or pursue their emotional feelings with less care of the verses. However, Du Fu made a lot of exploration and bold innovation and gave full play to the aesthetic strengths of the verses. Precise, changeable in the syntax, his poems were often deep in meaning and especially his preference to the use of contrast between positive and negative phases added more imagery and richer

- 《杜甫暮归诗帖》苏轼（北宋）
Copybook of Du Fu's Poems, by Su Shi (Northern Song Dynasty, 960-1127)

杜甫最擅长并且成就最高的是律诗。在他之前，律诗大多是酬赠应制之作，而杜甫用律诗反映了更为广阔的社会生活。写律诗因为要严守格律，诗人们要么难免落入卑琐庸俗，要么在意境胜出时往往无法兼顾格律，但杜诗则做了大量的探索和大胆的革新，充分发挥了律诗的美学特长。他的诗语言严谨，句法多变，含义深邃，尤其用正反相衬的手法，使诗的意象更加丰富，更富有层次。

杜甫的代表作《登高》，被誉为"古今七律第一"。

登 高

风急天高猿啸哀，渚清沙白鸟飞回。
无边落木萧萧下，不尽长江滚滚来。
万里悲秋常作客，百年多病独登台。
艰难苦恨繁霜鬓，潦倒新停浊酒杯。

杜甫写这首诗时，"安史之乱"已经结束四年了，但内乱四起，民不聊生。时世的苦难，家道的艰辛，个人的多病和壮志未酬，再加上好友李白等人的相继辞世，让他的心情无限沉重。为了排遣郁闷，他抱病登高远望。诗的前四句

factors and layers to the poems.

Du Fu's masterpiece *Climbing a Terrace* (*Denggao*) from *Eight Poems Written in Autumn* (*Qiuxing Bashou*) has always been known as the "First Place of Seven-*Lv*".

Climbing a Terrance

Wind blows high in the sky and monkeys cry;
Clear the islet with white sand where birds are wheeling;
Everywhere the leaves fall rustling from the trees,
While on forever runs the turbulent Yangtze River.
All around is autumnal gloom and I, far from home,
A prey all my life to ill health, climb the terrace alone;
Hating the hardships which have whiten my hair,
Sad that illness made me give up the solace of wine.

It was 4 years after the An-Shi Rebellion (755-762) when Du Fu wrote this poem, but civil strife was everywhere and people were in great hardship. Those sufferings, including difficult life, hardships of family and financial situations, his bad health and

勾画出一幅秋之图景。登上高处，感受大风呼啸，聆听空谷猿鸣，全诗便笼罩在悲凉的氛围之中。次句却平缓而出，水清沙白，飞鸟回旋，让人感到一种宁静的凄凉、空旷的惆怅。诗的三四两句，写出了落木萧萧的凄凉，滚滚江水的壮观，让人在悲伤中又生出壮心不已的豪情。于是引出后四句同样的境界："万里悲秋常作客"，是悲凉的进取；"百年多病独登台"，是命运的抗争。悲苦的命运固然是沉重感伤的，但也是丰富、深沉、有力度的。这首诗气象万千，状物抒情，达到了水乳交融、出神入化的境地，故被人称为登高绝唱。

broken dreams and together with the deaths of his friends including Li Bai made him even more frustrated. To distract depressed feelings, he climbed to the heights with illness and overlooked sceneries afar. The first four lines outlined a picture of autumn. The poet ascended to the heights, felt the wind whistling, listened to the ape's screams spreading in the empty Valley, all these set a desolate atmosphere. The second line was flat out and the clear water, white beaches and flying birds made people feel a quiet desolate and empty melancholy. The three and four lines presented the loneliness of falling leaves and the spectacular scene of turbulent Yangtse River, which aroused passion for dreams from grief. So the similar situation was led to the last four lines: "All around is autumnal gloom and I, far from home." It was the aspiration in grief; "A prey all my life to ill health, climb the terrace alone" was the fight against fate. While the misery fate was a heavy sentimental burden, it was rich, deep, and full of strength. Under a magnificent and changeful prospect, this poem was a perfect harmony of images and emotions, which created superb atmosphere and was known as the best poem of climbing heights.

● 杜甫草堂一隅
A corner of Du Fu's Thatched Cottage

> "诗魔"白居易

白居易（772—846），字乐天，号香山居士。他是中国历史上一位高产诗人，一生共写了三千多首诗，数量居唐朝诗人之冠。白居易酷爱写诗，笔耕不辍，甚至曾经

> "Poetry Wizard" Bai Juyi

Bai Juyi (772-846) whose courtesy name was Letian and self-titled name "Xiangshan Jushi" was a prolific poet in Chinese history. He wrote about over 3,000 poems, which ranked the highest among the poets in the Tang Dynasty. He ardently loved to write poems and was very diligent. He worked so hard at writing poems that he even had mouth sores and hands cocoon. In his later years, he also sorted his works and compiled collection of poems. At the same time, he pondered profoundly over poem theories. He was so obsessed with writing poems that he was like being pulled

• 白居易像
Portrait of Bai Juyi

- **杭州西湖白堤春色**

  白堤原名"白沙堤"，是唐时为贮蓄湖水灌溉农田而建，以风光旖旎著称。诗人白居易任杭州刺史时有诗云："最爱湖东行不足，绿杨荫里白沙堤。"指的就是此堤。堤上桃柳成行，芳草如茵，行人如入画中。

  Spring Scenery of the *Bai* (White) Causeway of West Lake in Hangzhou

  Bai Causeway, formerly known as "*Baisha* (White Sand) Causeway", was built for water storage and irrigation in the Tang Dynasty. It was famous for its beautiful scenery. When Bai Juyi was the provincial governor (*Cishi*) of Hangzhou, he wrote a poet and mentioned the causeway: "The scenery of East Bank makes me leave reluctantly. In the shade of aspens lies the *Bai* Causeway cozily." On the causeway, there were lines of peach and willow trees, as well as a carpet of green grass, which made the pedestrians seem to walk in a beautiful painting.

因为吟咏创作诗歌过度，导致口舌生疮、握笔的手指磨出了茧子。晚年时，他还将自己数量众多的作品进行分类整理，编成诗集。同时他对诗歌理论也有深刻的思考。他对写诗已经达到了"着魔"的地步，"酒狂又引诗魔发，日午悲吟到日西"，他用"诗魔"来形容自己写诗的冲动，所以后人称他为"诗魔"。

白居易是唐朝诗人中少有的既善于写诗，又在仕途发展上相对顺利的佼佼者。李白和杜甫虽然颇

by "magical" power, like "after getting drunk, he would keep writing poems a whole day long". So he described his impulse of writing poems as "Poetry Wizard", so did the people call him.

Bai Juyi was the few winners in the Tang Dynasty who was not only good at poems, but also did well in his political career. Li Bai and Du Fu, although quite talented, couldn't give full play to their talents in political circles. While Bai was working hard on poems and succeeded, his political career was also relatively smoothly and he was a high-level official

具才华，但在官场上却始终都郁郁不得志。而白居易在刻苦写诗、成绩斐然的同时，也在仕途上走得相对顺利，甚至一度担任过很高的官职，做了不少有利于民生的事，是一位深受百姓爱戴的好官。如今依然横贯杭州西湖之上的著名的"白堤"，就是他在当地为官时为了造福百姓所建造的。

白居易的诗平易浅近、通俗易懂，据说连乡下老妇人都能懂，是所有诗人中作品流传最广的。他的诗也深受外国人喜爱，比如在唐代时，白居易的诗就东渡日本、朝鲜，从朝廷到民间都广为传诵。中唐时的皇帝唐宣宗在《吊白居易》一诗中称赞说："童子解吟长恨曲，胡儿能唱琵琶篇。""长恨曲"和"琵琶篇"指的正是白居易最为著名的两首长篇叙事诗《长恨歌》和《琵琶行》，其中《长恨歌》流传最广。

《长恨歌》是一首以帝王和妃子为主角的长篇爱情叙事诗，描述了"中国四大美女"之一的杨贵妃与唐朝鼎盛时代"开元盛世"的缔造者唐玄宗之间荡气回肠的爱情故事。全诗讲述了杨玉环与李隆基从

once upon a time. Being an official, he did a lot of things conducive to people's livelihood, which won him deep support from the people. Now the "Bai Causeway" which still crosses the West Lake in Hangzhou City was built by him for the benefits of people there when he was a local official there.

Bai's poems were plain and easy to understand and it was said that even old rural women could understand. His poems were the most popular and widely circulated ones. They were also loved by foreigners. In the Tang Dynasty, they spread to Japan, Korea, from the court to the common people. Emperor Li Longji in the Tang Dynasty praised Bai in the poem *Condolence to Bai Juyi*: "Even little boys can recite *Song of Eternal Sorrow* and boys living in minority groups which are far away from central China can sing *Song of the Lute Player*". The two songs referred to the two most famous long narrative poems written by Bai Juyi.

Song of Eternal Sorrow was a long narrative love poem of emperor and a concubine. It described the soul-stirring love story between Imperial Concubine Yang who was one of "China's Four Beauties" and Emperor Li Longji

相遇相知并相恋到最后生死分离的整个过程，将两人爱情的轰轰烈烈表达得淋漓尽致。

长恨歌（节选）

汉皇重色思倾国，御宇多年求不得。
杨家有女初长成，养在深闺人未识。
天生丽质难自弃，一朝选在君王侧。
回眸一笑百媚生，六宫粉黛无颜色。
春寒赐浴华清池，温泉水滑洗凝脂。
侍儿扶起娇无力，始是新承恩泽时。
云鬓花颜金步摇，芙蓉帐暖度春宵。
春宵苦短日高起，从此君王不早朝。
承欢侍宴无闲暇，春从春游夜专夜。
后宫佳丽三千人，三千宠爱在一身。
金屋妆成娇侍夜，玉楼宴罢醉和春。
姊妹弟兄皆列土，可怜光彩生门户。
遂令天下父母心，不重生男重生女。

who created the peak time, Kaiyuan Flourishing Age. In the poem, the whole process in which Yang Yuhuan (Imperial Concubine Yang) and Li Longji (Emperor Li Longji) encountered, fell in love with each other and separated was introduced. It expressed their magnificent love vividly.

Song of Eternal Sorrow (Part)

Appreciating feminine charms, Emperor Li Longji sought a great beauty,
Throughout his empire he searched for many years without success.
Then a daughter of the Yang family matured to womanhood,
Since she was secluded in her chamber, none outside had seen her.
Yet with such beauty given by fate, how could she remain unknown,
One day she was chosen to attend the emperor.
Glancing back and smiling, she revealed a hundred charms,
All the ladies of the six palaces, at once seemed dull and colorless.
Approved to take a bath in Huaqing Spring at a cold spring night,

- 淡描青花唐明皇与杨贵妃故事图盘（清）
Light Sketched Blue-and-white Plate with Stories of Emperor Li Longji and Imperial Concubine Yang (Qing Dynasty, 1616-1911)

这段的诗意是：汉皇迷恋倾城倾国的美女，登基多年一直没找到中意的人。杨家有位刚长成的姑娘，养在深闺里没人见过。她天生丽质颇被珍惜，一天被选到皇上身边。她回头嫣然一笑百媚千娇，六宫施粉的妃嫔都黯然失色。春寒

《华清出浴图》康涛（清）

此图以杨贵妃出浴为主题，与《长恨歌》中"春寒赐浴华清池"的描写正相吻合。

Royal Bathing in Huaqing Spring, by Kang Tao (Qing Dynasty, 1616-1911)

With the theme of royal bathing of Imperial Concubine Yang, this painting echoed with the description in *Song of Eternal Sorrow*: "Approved to take a bath in Huaqing Spring at a cold spring night".

The warm water slipped down her glistening jade-like body.
When her maids helped her rise, she looked so frail and lovely,
At once she won the emperor's favor.
Her hair like a cloud and her face like a flower, a gold hair-pin adorning her tresses,
Behind the warm lotus-flower curtain, they took their pleasure in the spring night.
Regretting only the spring nights were too short and sun has risen,
He stopped attending court sessions in the early morning.
Constantly she amused and feasted with him,
Accompanying him on his spring outings, spending all the nights with him.
Though many beauties were in the palace, more than three thousand of them,
All his favors were centered on her.
Finishing her coiffure in gilded chamber, staying with him at night,
Feasting together in the marble pavilion, getting drunk in the spring.
All her sisters and brothers became nobles with fiefs,
How wonderful to have so much splendor centered in one family!
All parents of the world jealous of her family,
Wished for daughters instead of sons!

The meaning of the excerpt is as

料峭，杨贵妃得皇帝赐浴华清池，滑腻的温泉水洗过她那如凝脂的肌肤。侍女扶出，一副娇懒无力的媚态，这只是初承恩泽的时候。云一样的鬓发、花一般的容貌，头戴着金步摇，和皇帝在温暖的芙蓉帐里度过春宵。春宵苦短，太阳高升，从此君王不早朝。她备受宠爱，经常陪侍皇帝的宴席没有闲暇，不论春天游玩还是夜晚只有她在皇帝身旁。后宫美人三千人，君王对三千人的宠爱都集中在她一身。在华丽的宫殿里，她妆饰好了去伺候圣君，玉楼宴会后，君王和她醉倒进温柔乡里。姐妹弟兄都封了爵位，令人羡慕，一家门户生光。天下做父母的，都觉得生男儿还不如生个女郎。

这是《长恨歌》的第一部分，叙述了唐玄宗对杨贵妃的眷恋宠幸，为后文写二人之诀别、长恨作衬垫。

中国古代皇帝"后宫佳丽三千"，拥有无数的妃嫔，唐玄宗却独爱杨贵妃，甚至不理国家大事。诗人在描绘这段爱情的时候，极尽能事地渲染帝王贵妃之间的爱

follows: Emperor Li Longji was obsessed with beauties, but found none since his enthronement. Then a daughter of the Yang family was matured to womanhood, but nobody had ever seen her before. She was born beautiful and one day she was chosen to accompany the emperor. She was so charming and when she glanced back and smiled, all the other powdered ladies of the six palaces seemed dull and colorless at once. One cold spring, she was ordered to bathe in the Huaqing Spring. Her glistening jade-like body seemed too frail and lovely when the maids helped her in the bath. At once she won the heart of the emperor. Her hair was like a cloud and her face was like a flower. The gold hairpin was in her hair. Behind the warm lotus-flower curtain, they took their pleasure in the spring night. Spring night was too short, when the sun rose again, the emperor didn't want to attend court sessions any more. She was so favored by the emperor that she spent all the nights with him. All his favors were centered on her. No matter the imperial feasts or the spring outing, she was the only one who accompanied the emperor. She was so charming that she accompanied him at night. Feasting together in the marble pavilion, the

情的激荡起伏、山盟海誓。尽管历史上存在复杂的原因导致玄宗因为"安史之乱"而失去皇位，远逃四川，而当时许多人都将唐朝被叛军入侵，失去大片国土的原因归咎于杨贵妃。最后玄宗为平复众将怒气，不得不将贵妃赐死。杨贵妃成了玄宗昏庸误国的替罪羊。《长恨歌》的后半段着重渲染"长恨"的气氛中玄宗对贵妃的思念之情：这段感情不像天地那么长久，原来也

emperor inebriated with her. All her sisters and brothers became nobles with fiefs. How wonderful to have so much splendor! All parents wished to have daughters instead of sons!

This was the first part of *Song of Eternal Sorrow* which described Emperor Li Longji's favor for Imperial Concubine Yang. The first part formed an obvious comparison to the separation and eternal sorrow in the next parts.

Ancient Chinese emperors usually had numerous concubines in their palaces. While Emperor Li Longji loved Imperial Concubine Yang so much that he even ignored national affairs. In describing this, the poet tried his best to highlight the ups and downs of their love and their vows. Due to An-Shi Rebellion, the emperor lost his throne and escaped to Sichuan Province. Though there were complex reasons in history for the loss of throne, many people concluded that Imperial Concubine Yang should be responsible for the rebellion and land loss. At last, in order to ease the anger of people, the emperor ordered Yang death penalty. She became the scapegoat for the emperor's fatuous and stupid mistake. The last part of *Song of Eternal Sorrow* focused on the emperor's missing of her

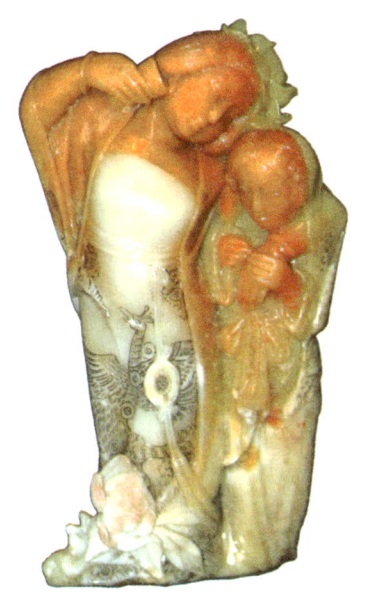

- 寿山石雕《贵妃醉酒》
  Shoushan Stone Carving of *The Drunken Beauty*

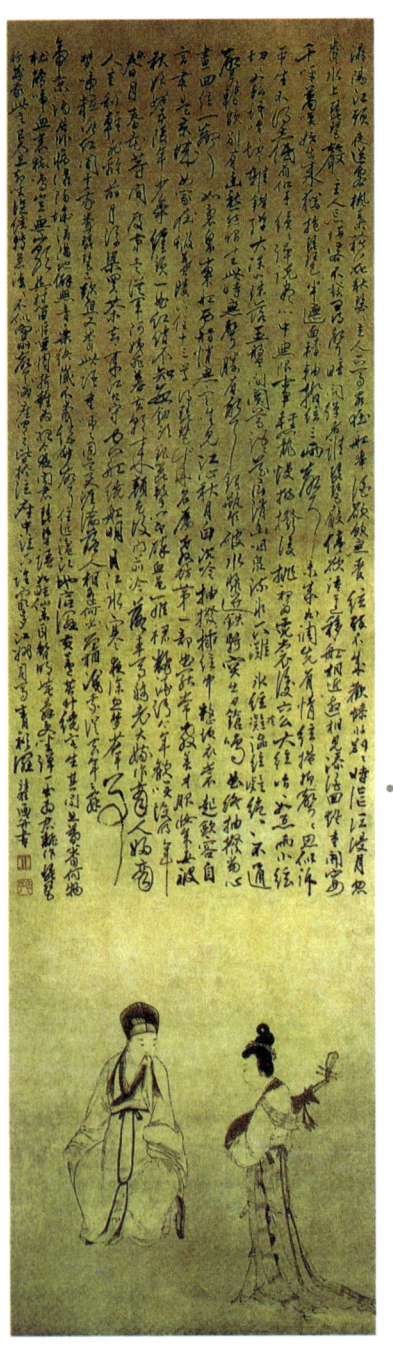

in the atmosphere of sorrow. The love was not eternal and there would be an end to it. While the sorrow regret and resentment would be everlasting and lingering around him, in which he could not stay together with the one he loved.

In *Song of Eternal Sorrow*, the poet did not directly criticize the rule of Emperor Li Longji's reign ironically, nor did he follow poets before him to claim

- 《琵琶行图轴》郭诩（明）

与《长恨歌》齐名的歌行体长诗《琵琶行》作于唐宪宗元和十一年（816）秋，时年白居易45岁，被贬官为江州司马。作品借描述弹琵琶歌伎的高超技巧和凄凉身世，抒发了作者个人受打击、遭贬斥的抑郁悲凄之情。在诗中，诗人把琵琶女视为自己的风尘知己，发出了"同是天涯沦落人，相逢何必曾相识"的慨叹，使作品具有不同寻常的感染力。

Scroll Painting of Song of the Lute Player (Pipa Xing), by Guo Xu (Ming Dynasty, 1368-1644)

The long narrative poem *Song of the Lute Player* which was as famous as *Song of Eternal Sorrow* was written in the lyric style in the autumn of the 11th year of Period Yuanhe (816), Tang Dynasty. Bai Juyi was at his age of 45 when he wrote it and he was demoted to the assistant prefecture chief of Jiangzhou (*Jiangzhou Sima*). In the poem, he portrayed a highly skilled lute player and her miserable experience and expressed his sorrows and depression caused by the demotion. He also viewed the lute player as his confidant and voiced his lament in the lines "We are both ill-starred, drifting in this world; No matter if we were strangers before this encounter." These lines added unusual infection to the poem.

会有尽头；不能和相爱之人长相厮守的这份怨念始终挥之不去。

《长恨歌》既没有直接批判讽刺玄宗的统治不善，沉溺玩乐，也没有像古人那样讽刺批判杨贵妃是"红颜祸水"，而是着重描写两人之间的真挚爱情。虽然玄宗为此付出了巨大的代价，带给国家沉痛的灾难，杨贵妃亦为此付出了生命，但或许正是因为如此，这段矢志不渝的爱情和这首荡气回肠的长诗才更加具有生命力和震撼力。这首诗千古传唱，里面的诗句脍炙人口，如最后四句"在天愿作比翼鸟，在地愿为连理枝。天长地久有时尽，此恨绵绵无绝期"，已经成为后世的痴男怨女们表达爱情的经典用语。

Yang as "Helen of Troy" (dangerous beauty). However, he focused on describing the true love between them. Although Emperor Li Longji paid great price and brought painful disaster to the country, Yang also lost her life. Perhaps due to it, the determined love and this soul-stirring poem gained even more vitality and power. This poem was read through the ages, and some of the well-known lines, such as the last four: "In heaven we shall be birds flying side by side; On earth we shall be twinned trunks tangling together. Heaven and earth may not last forever, but this sorrow is eternal." has become the classic love words for young men and women who are deeply in love to express their emotions.

> 王维

王维（701—761），字摩诘，是唐朝山水田园诗派的代表诗人，被后人称为"诗佛"。王维成就较高的诗歌作品都富有自然清净、远离世俗的超脱气息。

> Wang Wei

Wang Wei (701-761), with courtesy name as "Mojie", was the representative poet of the landscape and pastoral poetic school. He was respected as "Poetry Buddha" by later generations. And his famous poems were natural and pure and detached from worldly atmosphere.

In addition to writing poems, Wang's calligraphy and paintings were also very famous and he was proficient in music. Among poets in the Tang Dynasty, he was a versatile and all-round scholar. He combined music, calligraphy, painting and poems, which complemented each other. His poems tended to portray an

• 王维像
Portrait of Wang Wei

除了擅长写诗之外，王维的书法和绘画也非常有名，对音乐也很精通。在唐朝诗人之中，他称得上是多才多艺的全能文人。他将音乐、书法、绘画与诗歌融为一体，

atmosphere with colors like Chinese paintings, which would set people in the leisurely quiet natural world with birds twittering and flowers' fragrance after reading them. Also his landscape paintings reflected the poems'

- 《辋川图》 王维（唐）

  辋川位于今陕西省西安市南郊蓝田县的西南，是秦岭北麓的一条秀美川道。开元二十九年（741），王维40岁左右时在辋川买下了"蓝田别墅"，前后居住了将近14年。王维许多流传后世的山水田园诗都作于这一时期，他的诗集也命名为《辋川集》。

  Painting of Wangchuan, by Wang Wei (Tang Dynasty, 618-907)
  Wangchuan was located in southwest of Lantian County, southern suburbs of Xi'an City, Shaanxi Province. It was one beautiful river road in the north of Qinling Mountains. In the 29th year of Period Kaiyuan (741) in the Tang Dynasty, 40-year-old Wang Wei bought "Lantian villa" in Wangchuan and lived there for nearly 14 years. Many of his famous landscape and pastoral poems were written in this period of time. His verses' collections were also named *Wangchuan Anthology*.

互相配合，相得益彰。王维的诗句往往营造出山水画一般的色彩和意境，让人读过之后仿佛置身鸟语花香、悠然恬静的自然世界。而他的山水画中又能体现出诗句的意境，所谓"诗中有画，画中有诗"就是对王维诗画的最高评价。他也因其绘画才能而创造了水墨山水画派，被称为"南宗画之祖"。当时唐朝盛传"李白是天才，杜甫是地才，王维是人才"，可见王维的才华横溢是得到公认的。

王维虽然身居要职，但内心始终与世俗官场保持着一定的距离。他怀着一颗真正超脱的心来单纯地欣赏自然中的一草一木，并赋予它们禅意。他以淡泊的心态更多地关注山水田园的宁静淳朴之美，往往不惜笔墨描绘山水田园等自然景

atmosphere. So the judgment "poetic paintings, paintings in poems" was the highest praise of his poems and paintings. Benefiting from his painting skills, he started the Chinese Ink Landscape Art School and was also regarded as the "Founder of the Southern School of Chinese Landscape Art". It was said in the Tang Dynasty that "Li Bai is a genius, Du Fu is a talent and Wang Wei is a prodigy", showing that Wang's brilliance was recognized by people.

Though being an official, Wang Wei always kept certain distance with secular officialdom. He observed and appreciated the nature with his truly detached heart and entitled Zen to them. With a simple state of mind, he focused more on the pastoral beauty and mostly wrote poems of this theme. His poems created a quiet atmosphere away from the hubbub and

◆ 《山居图》唐寅（明）
Mountain Life, by Tang Yin
(Ming Dynasty, 1368-1644)

物，营造远离尘嚣的幽静氛围，反映出一种闲适清寂、隐逸出世的思想境界。后人因此皆推举王维为山水田园派的领军人物。

王维写作的最大特点就是用诗来营造画的意境，用看似平淡朴实的语言来表达富有哲理的思想和深厚的感情。

山居秋暝

空山新雨后，天气晚来秋。
明月松间照，清泉石上流。
竹喧归浣女，莲动下渔舟。
随意春芳歇，王孙自可留。

这首诗的前四句勾勒出一幅完美的山水画卷，展现出隐逸者梦寐以求的自然生活环境：幽静的山在雨后显得更加空灵，天气像晚来的秋天那样清爽怡然。明亮的月光从松树枝叶的缝隙中映照下来，若隐若现的清泉在石间流淌，发出清脆悦耳的流水之声。这样清幽脱俗的景象岂能不让人流连忘返？所以诗的最后一句"随意春芳歇，王孙自可留"表达出自己其实想要"留"的意愿。这个"留"不仅是想长住此地的意思，更是想要远离红尘喧

reflected a leisure hermit. Therefore, later generations all recognized Wang as the leader of the Landscape and Pastoral School.

The most distinct feature of his poetry-writing is using verse to build up a situation of painting, applying plain and simple language to express profound philosophy or deep emotions.

Autumn Evening in the Mountains

After fresh rain in quiet mountain,
Air is as fresh as the late autumn.
Among pine-trees bright moonbeams cast,
Crystal water flows on the stone.
Bamboo's whisper of washer-maids,
Lotus stirs when fishing boat wades.
Though fragrant spring may pass away,
Still here's the place for you to stay.

The first four lines outlined a perfect landscape, showing ideal natural living environment of hermits: Quiet mountains were even more ethereal after rain, the weather was fresh and clean like the late autumn. Bright moonlight came out through leaves of pine trees and clear water flowed over the crystal stones with a clear crisp sound of the water. How could people leave this quiet and refined beauty? So the last two lines "Though

嚣的愿望。而王维最矛盾的地方就在于此，与真正的隐士不同，他在实际生活中并未离开世俗，甚至在"安史之乱"时还被迫接受叛军授予的官职，尽管这只是无奈之举，但人生的这些无奈，让王维更加醉心于在诗画中营造自然纯净的心境。

fragrant spring may pass away, still here's the place for you to stay" expressed his wish to stay, which indicated not only to stay at this peaceful place but also to stay far away from this riproaring human world. However, he was contradicted in his heart. Different from real hermit, he never left the political circle in real life and was even forced to receive official position by the rebellion military during the An-Shi Rebellion. Though he could do nothing but accept it. At the same time, he indulged in pure state of mind created by poems and paintings, which was closely related with his belief on Buddhism.

• 三彩梳妆女坐俑（唐）
Three-color Sitting Clay Statue of a Dressing Woman (Tang Dynasty, 618-907)

> 李贺

　　李贺(790—816)，字长吉，是中唐时期一位独树一帜、才华横溢的诗人。他个性独特，风格鲜明，少年成名，英年早逝。在唐诗创作方面，李贺也是自成一派，在27年的短暂生命里创作出了颇具独特魅力的诗篇，奠定了他在诗坛不可取代的地位，与"诗仙"李白、晚唐时期的李商隐三人并

● 李贺像
Portrait of Li He

> Li He

Li He (790-816), whose courtesy name is Changji, is a unique, talented poet in the middle Tang Dynasty. With his distinctive personality style, he became famous at youth, but unfortunately suffered a premature death. In respect of the poetry creation, he had his own style and created a fairly unique charm of the poetries in his 27 years short life, which made him irreplaceable in poetic circles and along with Li Bai, "Poetry Immortal" and Li Shangyin of the late Tang Dynasty, he was known as one of "Three-Li" of the Tang Dynasty.

　　Li He, who was born in a run-down aristocratic family and very clever, could poetize when he was just 7 years old and was widely known because of his poetries at the age of 18. However, due to the unlucky fate, he could not

称唐代"三李"。

　　李贺出身于一个破落贵族之家，7岁能诗，聪颖过人，18岁时诗名远播。但由于命运的捉弄，数年后才在朝中谋得一个小官职，因地位卑微低下，尝尽人情冷暖，心情非常抑郁。仕途失意的他将满腔抱负都用在了诗歌创作上。传说他常常背一个破锦囊出游寻找灵感，想到一个妙句就写下投进囊中，归家后废寝忘食修改成诗。

　　李贺是中唐时期的浪漫主义诗人，又是中唐到晚唐时期诗风转变期的代表人物。他所写的诗大多慨叹生不逢时和内心苦闷，抒发对理想、抱负的追求，并且对当时藩镇割据、宦官专权和人民所受的残酷

just get a position, low and humble, in the imperial court until his middle age, which made him taste enough bitterness of the life and feel very depressed. Then the frustrated career path made him put all his ambitions on poetry creation. It was said that he usually went out with a shabby bag for inspiration, and when a good sentence came out, it would be written down and then casted into his bag. These sentences would be modified into poetries by his tireless work after he went home.

　　Li He was a Romantic poet in the Mid-Tang Dynasty and also a representative during the transition period of the poetic style from the Mid-Tang Dynasty to the late Tang Dynasty. Most of his poetries expressed his not being favored by chances, inner anguish and his pursuit of ideals and ambitions, and his poetries also reflected the independent rival principalities, eunuch dictator and the brutal deprivation which people were suffered from at that time.

• 彩色釉陶鍑（唐）
Color-glazed Clay Cauldron (Tang Dynasty, 618-907)

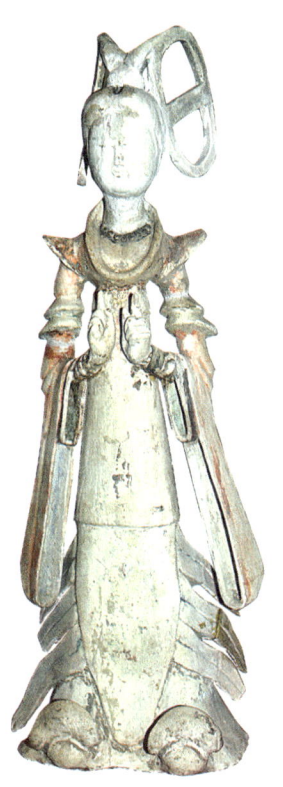

- 彩绘双环髻女立俑（唐）
  Color-painted Standing Clay Statue of a Woman with Double-bun (Tang Dynasty, 618-907)

He liked to write in the world of fairy tales and ghost stories. With his bold and tricky imagination, he created the erratic and flurried art realm to express his sentimental mood for the fast-going good time and time flies. His poetries were full of imagination, myths and legends and some words such as "death" and "blood" which were evasive words for many literati usually appeared in his poetries and also a lot of his poetries' contents took "ghost" as themes, which is a very different style with other poets in the Tang Dynasty. According to records, Li He was bony, fact tag and looks dark because of his perennial sick, thus he was called "Poetry Spirit".

Tomb of Su Xiaoxiao was one of Li He's poetries which took "ghost" as the theme. Su Xiaoxiao, a famous beauty in regions south of the Yangtze River, was talented and had superior skills, who became famous because of many literati's singing and praise in their works. After her death, people built a cenotaph for her at the lakeside of the West Lake of Hangzhou where many literati left their memorial poems to show their appreciation. However, Li He did exactly the unique way. He specifically wrote poetries to depict her tomb and her ghost,

剥削都有所反映。他喜欢在神话故事、鬼魅世界里驰骋，以其大胆、诡异的想象力，构造出波诡云谲、迷离惝恍的艺术境界，抒发好景不长、时光易逝的感伤情绪。他的诗富于想象，大量引用神话传说，还经常会出现"死""血"之类让一般文人避忌的字词，内容还有很多以"鬼"为题材,风格迥异于唐朝其他诗人。根据记载,李贺本人的长相也因常年病苦而瘦骨嶙峋、面容凹陷、气色暗沉,有"诗鬼"之称。

《苏小小墓》就是李贺"鬼"题材的诗篇之一。苏小小是江南名伎,才华出众,技艺超群,经许多文人墨客诗词歌咏而盛名远播。她死后,人们在杭州西湖畔为她建了一座衣冠坟墓,许多文人墨客都在墓旁留下纪念诗篇,以示赞赏。但李贺却另辟蹊径,不写苏小小的事迹,专门写诗描绘她的坟墓和她的鬼魂,营造出一种幽冥清冷的意境。

苏小小墓

幽兰露,如啼眼。

无物结同心,烟花不堪剪。

草如茵,松如盖,

风为裳,水为佩。

油壁车,夕相待。

冷翠烛,劳光彩。

西陵下,风吹雨。

全诗从坟墓的景色开始描绘,凄凉的景象加上丰富的联想,刻画出飘飘忽忽、若隐若现的苏小小鬼魂

creating a kind of ghosty and lonesome context rather than wrote her stories.

Tomb of Su Xiaoxiao

Dewdrops on the orchids in the shadow,
Like weeping eyes,
Finding naught to which to betroth your heart,
A haze of wild flowers unworthy of picking.
The grass is like a carpet,
The pine is like a canopy,
The wind is your clothes,
The water is your ornament.
In a varnished carriage,
Waiting all night.
Cold emerald light of the candles,
Flickering in vain.
Under the Xiling,
Wind blows the falling rain.

The poem began to depict from the scene of the tomb. The desolate scene and rich associates depicted an elusive and looming image of Su Xiaoxiao. The first sentence described Su Xiaoxiao's eyes with tears like dewdrops on the orchids. She was not able to fall in love with human being and she could just flutter lonely. The second sentence described her ghost image that grass would be her carpet, pines would be her canopy, wind would be her garment and water

• 杭州苏小小墓

苏小小墓位于杭州西湖西泠桥畔。传说苏小小死后葬于西泠桥畔，后人仰慕她的文采，在此建墓，墓前有石碑，上覆六角攒尖顶亭，叫作"慕才亭"，为前来吊唁的人遮蔽风雨。

Tomb of Su Xiaoxiao in Hangzhou City

The tomb of Su Xiaoxiao is located at the side of *Xiling* Bridge of West Lake in Hangzhou City. It was said that Su Xiaoxiao was buried at the side of *Xiling* Bridge after her death. The later generations admired her literary talent and built this tomb here. In the front of the tomb, there is a stone tablet covered with a pavilion with hexagonal points called "Admirer's Pavilion (*Mucai Pavilion*)" which is used to shelter people who come here to condole on Su Xiaoxiao from wind and rain.

的形象。第一句写到幽兰草带着露水，好像苏小小的幽灵眼含泪水。她不能再与人类相恋，只能孤独地飘荡。第二句写苏小小的幽灵形象，芊芊绿草做她的褥子，亭亭青松为她遮盖，春风做她的衣袂，流水做她的环佩。最后两句写苏小小生前乘坐的油壁车，如今还依然在等待着载她去幽会，只可惜她的情人已死，往日的幽会已成空。"西陵下"是苏小小与情人曾经约会的地方，如今风雨交加，两人都已不在人世。

这首诗塑造的女鬼并不是令

would be her jade. The last two sentences wrote the vanished carriage which was used by Su Xiaoxiao before her death were still waiting for her to dating, but unfortunately her lover had passed away and the old date was gone. "Under the Xiling" was the place where Su Xiaoxiao dated her lover, now it was windy and rainy because of their deaths.

　　The image of the female ghost shaped in this poetry was not very scary. It just restored the image of Su Xiaoxiao before her death which contained affection, tears and sadness, so it was a ghost with love and beauty. The poetry depicted Su Xiaoxiao in this way to

人害怕的形象，而是还原苏小小生前的风姿，有情有泪有悲伤，是爱与美的幽灵。诗人这样描写苏小小是想表达对生命的珍惜和对爱与美的追求。他怀才不遇，思想难免偏激，同时又富于想象，对人间现实社会感到绝望，便寄情于神仙鬼魅的世界，但却赋予它们人的温情和品性。即使是鬼魂，也带有李贺赋予的人性闪光点。

express his cherishment of life and pursuit of love and beauty. Li He was underappreciated and radical in thinking, meanwhile he was imaginative and felt desperate for the real society, thus he consoled himself by the world of fairy and ghost and gave them human feeling and character. Even though they were ghost, they also had the shining points of human being which were given by Li He.

> 孟浩然

孟浩然（689—740）和王维齐名，是唐代山水田园诗派的重要代表诗人，世称"王孟"。与王维不同的是，孟浩然一生没有出任任何官职。他也有过雄心壮志，不过在一次次碰壁之后，不得不彻底放弃

● 孟浩然像
Portrait of Meng Haoran

> Meng Haoran

Meng Haoran (689-740), as famous as Wang Wei, is also an important representative poet of landscape and pastoral poetic school in the Tang Dynasty. Wang Wei and Meng Haoran were called "Wang-Meng". However, being different with Wang Wei, Meng Haoran never got a position in imperial court in all his life. Once time he had some ambitions, however, after being frustrated again and again, he had to totally give up his career path and travel around, and then he started seclusion since he was 50 years old. Although in fact, his seclusion was forced by reality, he had the mood and temperament to be an recluse, which could be verified in his poetries.

The poetic conception of Meng Haoran was as simple as his pastoral life,

• 青花"踏雪寻梅"图罐（明）

据明代张岱的《夜航船》记载，孟浩然情怀旷达，常冒着大雪骑着驴寻找梅花，自称："吾诗思在灞桥风雪中驴背上。"这个典故常用来形容文人雅士赏爱风景、苦心作诗的情致。

Blue-and-white Pot with Pattern of "Searching Plum Blossom in Snow" (Ming Dynasty, 1368-1644)

According to *Night Boat* written by Zhang Dai in the Ming Dynasty (1368-1644), Meng Haoran was broad-minded and usually looked for wintersweets on his donkey in heavy snow, saying that: "My poetry is created on my donkey above the Bridge Ba in the wind and snow". This allusion is usually used to describe literati's temperament and interest in enjoying the view and writing the poems dedicatedly.

仕途，四处游历，并在50岁后隐居山林。虽然孟浩然的隐居其实是不得已而为之，但他却有着隐者的心境和气质，他的诗歌可以为证。

　　单纯的人生经历决定了孟浩然的诗歌意境和田园生活一样简单淳朴，浑然天成，不需雕饰。简单的社会关系也让孟浩然有更多的精力关注自我的意识和感受，诗歌内容自然也相对单一，主要强调自我。虽然孟浩然耐得住寂寞，甘心终生隐逸山林，但是作为儒家积极入世思想培养长大的知识分子，内心都免不了有追逐功名一展宏图的抱负和理想，过于清高自赏的性格让孟浩然宁可发出"恨无知音赏"的呼声，也不肯屈就现实，为自己争取机会。

　　孟浩然是唐代第一位倾大力写

being natural and not need to be modified, which was decided by his simple life experience. Since his social relations was simple, Meng Haoran put more attention to self-consciousness and self-feeling. The contents in his poetries were relatively simple and mainly emphasized oneself. Though Meng Haoran could bear the loneliness and would like to live in seclusion all life, as an intellectual cultivated by the thought of Confucian active involvement in world affairs, in his heart, he still held the ambitions and ideals to chase fame and get a prosperous future. However, his over-virtuous and self-appreciated character made him would rather shout out "It is regretful that there is no one who can understand me" than surrender to the reality to strive for a chance.

　　Meng Haoran was the first poet of the Tang Dynasty who made great

作山水诗的诗人，将南朝以来的山水诗提升到新的境界。他的诗绝大部分为五言短篇，多写山水田园和隐居的逸兴以及羁旅行役的心情。其中虽不无愤世嫉俗之词，而更多属于诗人的自我表现。他善于发掘自然和生活之美，即景会心，写出一时真切的感受，自然浑成，而意境清幽。

或许正是由于孟诗的语言单纯，通俗易懂，他的许多脍炙人口的作品都是中国儿童初读唐诗时必修的功课。比如有名的《春晓》就朗朗上口，容易记忆，是孩子们喜欢吟咏、能够快速背诵的唐诗之一。

春 晓

春眠不觉晓，处处闻啼鸟。
夜来风雨声，花落知多少。

这首诗是孟浩然隐居在湖北襄阳的鹿门山时所作，意境自然优美。他通过早晨睡醒起来一念之间想起的景象，联想到美好的画面，生动地表达出对春天的热爱和怜惜之情。此诗没有直接描绘春天，而是通过自己的听觉感受和联想捕捉春天的气息，表达自己钟爱春天的

efforts to write landscape poetries and promoted the poetries since the Southern dynasties (420-589) to a new level. Most of his poetries were five-character short story, mostly describing his enjoyment in landscape, seclusion and traveling. Although there were some cynical words, more words were the poet's self-expression. He was good at exploring the beauty of nature and life. When he saw any beauty, he wrote down his real feelings in time, making his poetries natural, quiet and beautiful.

Perhaps just because the language in his poetries was simple and easy to understand, a lot of his works were the compulsory course for Chinese children when they came to contact with poetries of the Tang Dynasty. For example, the famous poetry *Spring Morning* was catchy and easy to remember, which made it become one of poetries of the Tang Dynasty children like to read and quickly recite.

Spring Morning

This spring morning in bed I'm lying,
Not to awake till birds are twittering.
After last night of wind and showers,
How many are the fallen flowers.

怜惜之情。一句"处处闻啼鸟"就把热闹的场面形象地勾画出来，抓住了春天万象更新、充满活力的特征。正是这可爱的春晓景象，使诗人很自然地联想到：昨夜我在蒙眬中曾听到一阵风雨声，现在庭院里盛开的花儿到底被摇落了多少呢？虽然风雨并不会破坏春天的景象，

This poetry was written by Meng Haoran when he lived in seclusion in Lumen Mountain which was located in Xiangyang of Hubei Province, in which artistic conception was very natural and beautiful. By a glimpse of an imaginative scene came out to his mind when he woke up in a morning, he associated a beautiful picture to express his feelings and cherishment to spring. Although no direct description of spring appeared in this poetry, the spring was written through the poet's auditory sense and association to express his love and cherishment. A lively scene was vividly sketched out by the sentence "Not to awake till birds are twittering" which grasped the undated and dynamic characteristics of spring. It was just the lovely scene of spring morning that made the poet naturally associate that: Last night, I had indistinctly heard the sound of wind and shower, now in the courtyard how many blooming flowers after all had been fallen down? Although the weather would not damage the scene of spring, the fallen flowers gained people's pity. Thus

- 《亭树春晓图》黄宾虹（近代）
  Pavilion and Trees in Spring Morning, by Huang Binhong (Modern Times)

但是摇落了花瓣，又让人不禁怜惜。"花落知多少"隐含着诗人对春光流逝的淡淡哀怨以及无限遐想。全诗贴近生活，情景交融，意味隽永，读起来又朗朗上口，通俗易懂，因此深受人们的喜爱。

the poet's light sadness and unlimited imagination to the fast going spring time was implicated in the sentence "How many are the fallen flowers". The whole poetry was close to life, rich in scenes, timelessly meaningful, easy to read and sing, clear and understandable, so it was very popular.

孟浩然与唐玄宗

据说孟浩然有一次在王维家做客，恰逢唐玄宗微服私访也来探望王维，孟浩然情急之下躲到床底。皇帝看出王维在跟人喝酒，便问起此人。王维说他是一介平民，不敢面见皇上，躲起来了。唐玄宗想，王维的朋友多半也是有才之人，就请他出来见见。孟浩然自报家门后，玄宗得知他就是写出《春晓》一诗的孟浩然，很是赞赏，命令他当场作诗。孟浩然一时着急，就把刚才喝酒时打的腹稿《岁暮归南山》吟出，其中有一句"不才明主弃，多病故人疏"，谦称自己才华不够，所以不为圣明皇上赏识。唐玄宗听了很不高兴，觉得孟浩然满腹牢骚，在埋怨皇帝不识人才，从此孟浩然的仕途之路也就断送了。

Meng Haoran and Emperor Li Longji

It was said that once when Meng Haoran was visiting Wang Wei at his home, unexpectedly, Emperor Li Longji came by in private, too. Meng Haoran was so hurry that he hid under the bed. Emperor found that Wang Wei was drinking with somebody, so he asked who that was. Wang answered that the man who drinking with him was just a civilian and did not dare to meet the emperor and hid himself. Emperor thought that if the man was Wang Wei's friend, he mostly could be a talented one, so he asked for meeting this man. After Meng Haoran stating his name, Emperor Li Longji knew that he was just the one who wrote *Spring Morning*, so he showed a great appreciation to Meng, and asked him to make a poem on site. Meng Haoran was so anxious that he recited the poetry *On Returning at the Year's End to Zhongnan Mountain* which was drafted in mind when he was drinking just now, in which there was a sentence "Banished for my blunders by a wise ruler, and avoided by my friends for my sickness" that humbled himself that he was not talented enough to get the wise emperor's appreciation. After hearing that, Emperor Li Longji was very unhappy, thinking that Meng was very disgruntled and complaining that emperor could not spot the talent. Since then Meng Haoran's career path was completely ruined.

> 王昌龄

王昌龄（？—约756），字少伯，是盛唐时期边塞诗派的重要代表人物。他的七绝诗独步诗坛，只有李白可以与他媲美，所以后人又尊称他为"七绝圣手"。王昌龄出身低微，直到中年才考中进士谋得官职，但此后官运并不顺利，几经浮沉，曾经被贬谪到唐朝西北边境地区。边塞土地辽阔、风光壮美、气势雄浑，又逢唐朝此时在边境驻守重兵，战事频繁。他亲身经历边塞生活，于是创作出许多以军旅生活为题材的著名边塞诗篇。在人才济济、群星闪耀的盛唐时期，王昌龄与高适、岑参等人将视野扩展到边疆，在诗中描写边塞风光，带有大漠苍茫的气势，风格独树一帜，自成边塞诗派。尤其王昌龄的边塞诗格调高昂、士气雄壮，所作

> Wang Changling

Wang Changling (?-approx.756) with courtesy name Shaobo, is an important representative figure of frontier fortress poetic school in the blooming Tang period. His seven-*Jue* poetry was unconquerable in poetic circles and only Li Bai could compare with him, hence, he was called "Best in Seven-*Jue* Poetry" by later generations. He was born humbly and could not be a *Jinshi* (a successful candidate in the highest imperial examinations) and got a position in the imperial court until his middle age. However, after that his career prospect did not go smoothly, after several ups and downs, he was once demoted and sent to the northwest frontier of the Tang Dynasty, which was extensive, beautiful, grand and magnificent. At the same time, a lot of station troops were sent by the Tang Dynasty and wars

• 汉长城玉门关

玉门关故址在今甘肃敦煌西北小方盘城。当时中原与西域交通莫不取道此处，因此它是汉代重要的军事关隘和丝绸之路交通要道。

Yumen Pass of the Great Wall in the Han Dynasty

The former location of Yumen Pass is in present Xiaofangpan Town of Dunhuang, Gansu Province. At that time, the transportation between Central Plains and the Western Regions had to be via this place, so it was an important military gate and the vital communication line of the Silk Road in the Han Dynasty (206 B.C.-220A.D.).

frequently happened. He experienced frontier life by himself, hence creating a lot of famous frontier fortress poetries which took military life as themes. In the prosperous period of the Tang Dynasty, there were a galaxy of talents among which Wang Changling, Gao Shi, Cen Shen and others extended vision to the frontier. In their poetries, the view of frontier fortress was portrayed in great momentum; the style was set up a new banner being Frontier Fortress Poetic School. Among the poetries, in particular, the style of frontier fortress poetries made by Wang Changling was high and morale was magnificent. His poetry *On the Frontier* had been well-known since then and was the treasure of the poetries of the Tang Dynasty, also was praised as the grand finale in seven-*Jue* poetry of the Tang Dynasty.

《出塞》纵横古今，是唐朝诗歌中的珍品，被誉为唐人七绝诗中的压卷之作。

出 塞

秦时明月汉时关，万里长征人未还。
但使龙城飞将在，不教胡马度阴山。

On the Frontier

The moon and the Pass of the Qin and Han dynasties,

这首诗前两句的意思是：几百年以前的秦朝、汉朝时的明月和边关还在那里，没有改变，而这明月下的边关所发生的战争却从来没有停止过。有多少人战死沙场，又有多少战士仍然戍守着边关，不能回家。诗人的想象穿越时空回到几百年以前的秦汉，追忆从那时开始就战事不断的边关，直到唐朝也依然不能安宁。月亮和边关不会随着时间而改变，但是为了保卫家园而参战的士兵多少年来前仆后继，在不断地变换。他们常年驻守边关，不能回家，甚至死在战场，而边塞地区百姓的生活也不得安宁。诗人只用两句14个字就把塞外连年不休的惨烈战事勾勒了出来，让人们读后自然而然地联想到冷月照边关的苍凉景象。

后两句的意思是：如果汉朝镇守龙城边关、战无不胜的"飞将军"李广还活着就好了，他不会让匈奴的骑兵跨过边关所在的阴山，侵犯大唐、破坏百姓的家园。事实上，虽然唐朝当时一直派重兵镇守西域和边关，但是由于匈奴等游牧民族灵活机动，经常攻打一阵之后就逃跑，不断骚扰。而且西域的丝

And the road our troops are travelling goes back three hundred miles.
For the Winged General at the Loong City,
That never a Tartar horseman might cross the Yin Mountains.

The meaning of the first two sentences is that: The moon and the frontier junctures of the Qin Dynasty and Han Dynasty were still there, and nothing changed. While under the moon, wars at the border were never stopped. How many people had died on the battle felids and how many soldiers were still there for guarding the frontier junctions and could not go home? The poet's imagination traveled through time and space back to the Qin and Han dynasties hundreds years ago, recalling that the wars at the frontier junctures were started then and lasting until the Tang Dynasty. The moon and the frontier junctures would never changed over time, but the soldiers coming here for fighting for their homeland for years were constantly changing. They defended the frontier junctures throughout the year and could not go home, even died on the battle fields, and people in the frontier fortress had also no peace. It was just the 14 words used by the poet that sketched out the brutal wars running in the frontier fortress for years from which people would naturally associate the desolate view that the cold moon was shining the border.

The meaning of the last two sentences is that: It would be good that if Li Guang, the invincible"Winged General"guarding the frontier juncture the Loong City in the Han Dynasty, was still alive, he would never let the Hans' cavalries come across the Yin Mountains in which the frontier juncture was to intrude the Tang Dynasty and destroy people's homes. In fact, even though a large number of troops were sent all along to guard the Western Regions and the frontier junctures in the Tang Dynasty, due to the flexibility of the nomadic people such as the Hans who usually attacked just for a while and then ran and then came and go again and again. Moreover, the Silk Road of the Western Regions was the transportation thoroughfare between the Tang Dynasty and Central Asia, and other places for trade contacts down the ages. The valuable goods and properties attracted many robbers, bandits, and also made the small countries around it wanted to control it. So over the years, governing

绸之路自古是唐朝与中亚等地进行贸易往来的运输要道，贵重的货物财物吸引来许多强盗、土匪，也令周边的小国对这条商贸要道的控制权垂涎三尺。所以多年来，治理和守卫西域边关一直是唐朝皇帝最关心也很头痛的事情。尽管在盛唐时期，唐朝因为军力强大，一度扩大

- **西汉名将李广**

  李广（？-前119），陇西成纪（今甘肃静宁西南）人，西汉时期的名将。他连年领兵抗击匈奴，被称为"飞将军"。

  Famous General Li Guang of the Western Han Dynasty (206 B.C.-25A.D.)

  Li Guang (?-119 B.C.), born in Chengji of Longxi (present in the southwest of Jingning, Gansu Province) was the famous general in the Western Han Dynasty. Year after year, he led the army to resist the Huns and was called "Winged General".

了对西域的统治范围，但同时也延长了边关的战线，并为此耗费了巨大的开销补给军队，导致边关人民的生活贫穷困苦，不堪重负。《出塞》这首诗直接表现出了诗人对朝廷用人不当和将领们昏庸无能的不满。诗人希望当朝能够出现像汉代大将李广那样能力挽狂澜的将领，可以彻底打败外敌，早日平息边塞战事，让百姓能够过上安定的生活。

and guarding the frontier juncture of the Western Regions was always the most concerned and worried issue of the emperors of the Tang Dynasty. Although in the Prosperous Period of the Tang Dynasty, due to the strong military power, the scope of government for the Western Regions had been expanded for a time in the Tang Dynasty, but at the same time, the front of the frontier juncture was extended, which cost a huge number of money for supporting the military, resulting that people there were in poverty and hardship and not able to afford the burden. *On the Frontier* directly expressed the poet's dissatisfaction for the improper use of the people used by the imperial court and fatuity and incompetence of the generals. The poet hoped that in the current imperial court, there would be a competent general like Li Guang, a general in the Han Dynasty, who could turn back the powers of darkness and thoroughly defeated the enemies and settled down the wars in the frontier fortress as soon as possible, so that people could live a stable life.

> 杜牧

杜牧（803—852），字牧之，号樊川居士，生于诗书官宦之家，祖父杜佑是唐代著名的政治家、史学家，先后任三朝宰相，一生好

● 杜牧像
Portrait of Du Mu

> Du Mu

Du Mu (803-852) with courtesy name Muzhi was self-titled Fanchuan Jushi and born in Courtiers Family of poetry. His grandfather Du You was a famous statesman, historian and served as minister for three dynasties of the Mid-Tang Dynasty who was studious all his life and very erudite and written two hundred volumes of *Tong Dian*. The deep and strong family study tradition and excellent family life made Du Mu graceful and self-confident, knowledgeable and versatile. He was not only proficient in all kinds of literature creation, but also good at handwriting and painting. When he was 20 years old, he had been very learned and his works had been widely read by scribes. Even there were some celebrities of that time who directly recommended Du Mu to the

学，博古通今，著有《通典》二百卷。深厚的家学传统和优越的家庭生活，让杜牧自信洒脱，博学多才，不仅文学创作样样精通，还擅长书法、绘画。杜牧20岁时，已经博古通今，作品被文士们广为传诵，甚至有当时的知名人士向主考官直接推荐他，最终杜牧还是靠自己的才华，在26岁的时候进士及第，并顺利获得官职。

杜牧尤其喜欢研究军事，经常公开表达自己的政治见解，表现出过人的才华。然而他生不逢时，

examiner, however, finally he got into the top 3 at his 26 years old on his own and then smoothly got a position.

Du Mu especially liked to study military and often openly expressed his political opinions, showing the extraordinary talent. However, he was not favored by chances, even though he was familiar with history and gained an insight into the current situation, he was not able to turn back the powers of darkness for the weak situation of the late Tang Dynasty, thus he had no choice but to put all grief and anger to the loose life. Du Mu's loose was well-known at that time, especially when he was in the prosperous city Yangzhou, he almost went to brothels to look for fun every day, which was also put in his poetry by him: "I awake, after dreaming ten years in Yangzhou, known as fickle, even in the Street of Blue Houses"

Du Mu wrote a large number of past-cherishing poetries, thinking of the past and using ancient things to satirize the present. His past-cherishing poetries

- 《元曲选》中的版画 "杜牧之诗酒扬州梦"
  Print of *Du Mu's Dream of Poetry and Wine in Yangzhou*, from *Collections of Yuan Qu*

虽然熟读史书，看透时局，但面对日薄西山的晚唐局势也无法力挽狂澜，只能无奈地将一腔悲愤交于酒肆歌楼。杜牧的风流在当时非常有名，尤其身处当时繁华的扬州时，他几乎日日流连青楼，寻欢作乐。他自己也写诗说："十年一觉扬州梦，赢得青楼薄幸名。"

杜牧写了大量怀古诗，怀念过去，以古讽今。他的怀古诗富有感情，又精于用典，具有很高的水平。杜牧写诗善用七言绝句，篇幅短小精悍，表达感情明亮爽快。由于杜牧的诗歌成就卓然，后人尊称杜牧为"小杜"，有别于前人杜甫。而晚唐又以杜牧和李商隐的成就最大，人称李商隐为"小李"，有别于前人李白。所以后人合称二人为"小李杜"，以此表示对他们成就的肯定。杜牧和李商隐也是惺惺相惜的好友，彼此之间互相赠诗。两人诗风不尽相同。如果说杜牧的诗风偏刚性的豪迈清爽，那么李商隐的诗风就是偏柔性的凄美婉约。

杜牧的怀古诗中最有名的当数《赤壁》，它不仅是一首优秀的七

were full of emotions and proficient in the use of allusions, which was at a very high level. He was good at writing seven-*Jue* poetry which had few words and bright and lively emotions. Due to Du Mu's achievement in poetries, he was called "Little Du (*Xiao Du*)" which was to differentiate with predecessor Du Fu. And the most achievements in the late Tang Dynasty were belong to Du Mu and Li Shangyin, so Li Shangyin was called "Little Li (*Xiao Li*)" which was to differentiate with predecessor Li Bai. Therefore, they were called together "Little Li and Du (*Xiao Li Du*)" by later generations to confirm their achievements. Du Mu and Li Shangyin also appreciated each other and presented poetries to each other. Their poetic styles were different, and if Du Mu's was harder, bold and refresh, Li Shangyin's was softer, sad and graceful.

Red Cliff was the most famous poetry of his past-cherishing poetries which was not only an excellent seven-*Jue* poetry, but also showed his military talent. In particular, the famous and classic "Battle of Red Cliff" in history was used in this poetry as an allusion to express his ideas, which triggered people's broader and more diversified thinking.

绝诗，还表现了杜牧的军事才能，尤其诗中使用中国历史上著名的经典战役"赤壁之战"作为典故来表达思想，引发了人们更广阔和多元化的思考。

赤壁

折戟沉沙铁未销，自将磨洗认前朝。
东风不与周郎便，铜雀春深锁二乔。

前两句诗的大概意思是：一支

Red Cliff

*The broken spear still unrusted in the sand,
I have burnished the symbol of an ancient kingdom.
Except for east wind aiding General Zhou Yu,
Spring would have sealed both Qiao sisters in Copper Bird Palace.*

The general meaning of the first two sentences is that: A broken spear sunk in the sand of the water, buried but not totally rusted. After being got out and

- 赤壁之战
  Battle of Red Cliff

铜戟（东汉）
Copper halberd (Eastern Han Dynasty, 25-220)

折断的铁戟沉在水底沙中，被掩埋着还没有完全被腐蚀掉。打捞出来后，经过打磨清洗，发现这是三国时期赤壁之战所遗留下来的武器。这一句从一支折断的旧戟引起赤壁之战的话题，转而引导读者回忆起赤壁之战。第三、第四句诗转而讨论"周瑜借东风"的历史典故：假如当年周瑜不借助东风火烧曹操的连锁战船，决定性地扭转战局，结果恐怕是曹操取胜。而周瑜的妻子小乔和孙策的妻子大乔就会被俘虏，成为曹操的小妾了。这首七绝怀古诗一反常人思维，令人耳目一新。

washed and polished, it was found that it was a weapon left from the Battle of Red Cliff in the Three Kingdoms Period (220-280). This sentence led to the topic of the Battle of Red Cliff from a broken spear and then recalled readers' memories of the battle. The third and the fourth sentences turned to discuss the history allusion "Zhou Yu borrowed the east wind": If Cao Cao's chain warships had not been burned by Zhou Yu who was aided by the east wind which decisively reversed the situation, probably the battle would have been ended with Cao Cao's victory. And Zhou Yu's wife, Xiaoqiao and Sun Ce's wife Daqiao would be captured and became Cao Cao's concubines. This past-cherishing seven-*Jue* poetry was different from others which adopted the normal perspectives and presented a new one.

赤壁之战与借东风

汉献帝建安十三年（208）七月，曹操率领水陆大军，号称百万，发起荆州战役，讨伐盘踞东吴的孙权。孙权和刘备组成联军，由周瑜指挥，在长江赤壁（今湖北赤壁市西北，一说今嘉鱼东北）一带大破曹军，从此奠定了三国鼎立格局。这是中国历史上一场著名的以少胜多的战役。此战之后，天下三分的雏形开始形成，问鼎江山的角逐拉开了新的序幕。传说赤壁之战中，孙刘联军主将周瑜利用东风骤起，出其不意火烧曹操的水军战船，从而取得战役的决定性胜利。

Battle of Red Cliff and Borrowing East Wind

In July of the 13th year of Jian'an Period (208), in the reign of Emperor Liu Xie, Cao Cao led his army and navy known as one million soldiers to launch the battle of Jingzhou in order to suppress the Kingdom of Wu ruled by Sun Quan who, together with Liu Bei, composed an united army commanded by Zhou Yu. They defeated Cao Cao's army in the area of Red Cliff along the Yangtze River (present in the northwest of Chibi City, Hubei Province; another version says it's in the northeast of present Jiayu), establishing the pattern of the three Kingdoms since then, which was also a famous battle of using the few to defeat the many in Chinese history. After this battle, the prototype of dividing the world in three began to form and the new prelude of fighting for winning the world had been on. It was said that in the Battle of Red Cliff, Zhou Yu, the commanding general of the united army, made excellent use of the time when the east wind arrived, unexpectedly burned Cao Cao's navy warships and won the decisive victory in the battle.

• 东吴统帅周瑜
Zhou Yu, Commander of the Kingdom of Wu

> 李商隐

李商隐（约813—约858），字义山，号玉谿生，是唐诗在晚唐时期最后辉煌的代表诗人。李商隐从小家境贫寒，很幸运得到"牛党"的贵族令狐楚的悉心栽培和大力帮助，并且顺利出任官职。而他却偏偏娶了"李党"成员王茂元的女儿为妻，并且与妻子王氏感情融洽美满，因而遭到牛党的排斥。此后，李商

- 李商隐像
  Portrait of Li Shangyin

> Li Shangyin

Li Shangyin (approx. 813-858) whose courtesy name is Yishan, self-titled Yuxisheng, was a representative poet of the last resplendence of Tang poetry in the late Tang Dynasty. Li Shangyin's family was poor when he was young, but he was luckily appreciated and helped greatly by the noble of Niu Clique, Linghu Chu. Li was successfully appointed as an official. However, Li married the daughter of Wang Maoyuan, who is a member of Li Clique. What's more, Li Shangyin and his wife were very sweet and loved each other, so he was excluded by Niu Clique. From then on, Li Shangyin had to make his living difficultly in the fight between Niu and Li Cliques, and floundered everywhere among the local governments, attached to them, acting as their support staff, while

隐便在牛李两党争斗的夹缝中求生存，辗转于各藩镇充当幕僚，郁郁而不得志，后潦倒终身。李商隐创作的名噪一时、备受人们追捧的爱情诗中，有很多诗篇都是关于他早亡的妻子王氏的。他的诗贴近人们内心最普遍共通的情感诉求，更能表达普通大众的思想感情，获得了百姓们的欢迎，在民间被阅读和传诵的普及率相当高。

李商隐的诗虽然不及李白、杜甫和白居易等人的诗有名，但他却是对后世最有影响力的唐代诗人。爱好李商隐诗的人比爱好李白、杜甫、白居易诗的人更多，这与他诗中透露出的至情至性有关。他最负盛名的代表作《锦瑟》就可以让读者深刻地感受到李商隐爱情诗的魅力。

锦　瑟

锦瑟无端五十弦，一弦一柱思华年。
庄生晓梦迷蝴蝶，望帝春心托杜鹃。
沧海月明珠有泪，蓝田日暖玉生烟。
此情可待成追忆，只是当时已惘然。

诗的前两句写古琴无来由地有着五十根琴弦，这每一条弦所发出

he felt depressed for his lost dream and lived a poor life thereafter. Li Shangyin is famous for his love poems and they are pursued by people, among which many are about his wife Wang who died early. His poems are close to the most common emotion appealing and can express ordinary people's minds and sentiments, so they are welcomed by the civilians and are widely read and recited.

Although Li Shangyin's poems are not as high as those of Li Bai, Du Fu and Bai Juyi, he is the poet of Tang poetry who has the most influence on the afterworld because people who are fond of Li Shangyin's poems are more than those who like Li Bai, Du Fu, and Bai Juyi's poems, which is related with the thoughts and emotions expressed by his poems. His most well-known representative work, *The Gorgeous Harp (Jin Se)*, can let people experience the charm of Li Shangyin's love poems.

The Gorgeous Harp

I wonder why the gorgeous harp has fifty strings,
Every string reminds me my flower-like youth.
The sage Zhuangzi was day-dreaming bewitched by butterflies,
The spring-heart of Emperor Wang is

的每一个音符，都让听到的人觉得怅然若失。弹奏出的乐曲听上去都是悲伤的声音，让人不禁想起过去那些美好的日子。第三、第四句诗用了庄子梦到自己变成蝴蝶，望帝死后化身杜鹃的神话传说来营造一种虚幻的境界，象征诗人在追忆中如梦似幻的心境，表达内心对爱情的坚定追求如杜鹃泣血一般，用情不悔。第五、第六句描绘古琴的声音如歌如泣，让人联想到明月下沧海中，泪水化作粒粒珍珠的图景；

expressing in a cuckoo.
Mermen weep their pearly tears down the broad sea,
Lantian is breathing its jade under the warm sun.
And the moment ought to have lasted forever,
Has come and gone before I knew.

In the first two sentences, the ancient harp has fifty strings without reasons. Each note enunciated by the string will make people feel that they have lost something. The music sounds sad, making

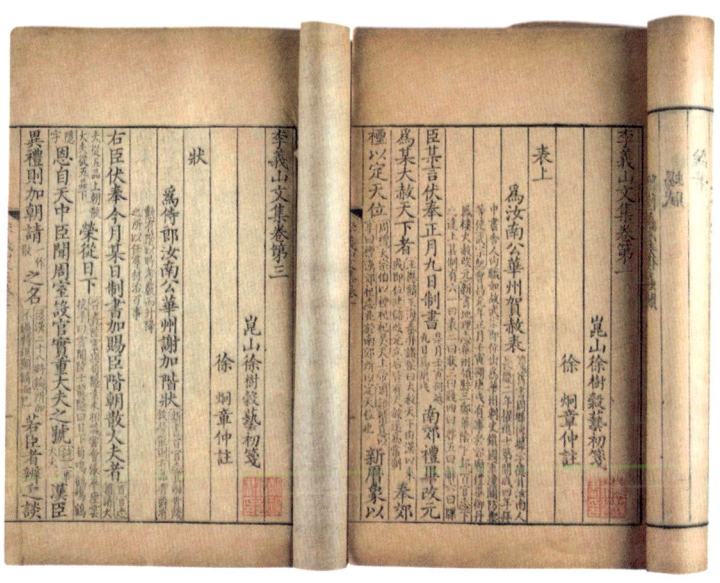

• 《李义山文集》书影
Sample Copy of *The Collections of Li Yishan*

又如蓝田暖阳高照，由玉而升起的轻烟缥缈朦胧。诗人在琴音缭绕中追忆往事，人生的种种际遇历历在目，哀怨、清寥、缥缈……最后一句是点睛之笔，将这种感受推向高

people think of the past happy days. The third and fourth sentences use the stories Zhuangzi dreaming to be a butterfly and Emperor Wang becoming a cuckoo after death to create a kind of unreal state, which symbolize the poet's dream-like mood and express that his inner pursuit of love is as firm as the crying cuckoo with blood, never regretting his love. The fifth and sixth sentences describe the voice of the ancient harp as melody and makes people think of the tears turning into pearls in the deep sea under the bright moon and the hazy smoke rising from the jades under the warm sun. The poet recalled the past things with the melody, during which the experience of his life was seen again, sadness, loneliness, confusing all around the heart. The last sentence is the highlight, pushing this feeling to the highest: One day the true feelings will be memory. Just like today

- **湖南长沙马王堆汉墓出土的鼓瑟乐俑**
  瑟是中国古代的一种拨弦乐器，最早的瑟有50根弦，故又称"五十弦"。后来逐渐演变为25根弦，弦的粗细不同，每弦有一柱。

  Clay Statue of a Musician Playing Musical Instrument (*Se*), excavated from the Mawangdui Tomb, in Changsha City, Hunan Province
  Se is a plucked string musical instrument in ancient China. The earliest *Se* had fifty strings, so it was called "Fifty-string" as well. Later it was changed into twenty-five strings. The thickness of the strings was different, and each string had one pillar.

潮：这份真情有一天也会成为回忆，就如同今日追忆过去，依旧感到刻骨铭心的痛楚；只是当年没有好好珍惜，一切都已经无法回到过去了。可叹人生如梦，往事如烟，佳人不再。最后两句诗表现了诗人内心无限的哀怨，那种怅惘的苦痛郁结于心，久久不退。

　　这首诗表达的是李商隐对亡妻最深沉的思念，想起和妻子在一起的美好岁月，如今却难再相伴的悲痛之情。根据诗句字面的意思，也可以理解成对青春逝去的人生感慨，还可以看作对自己某段人生经历的思考和叹息。这三种解释的基调都是一种曾拥有过却失去，难再拥有的伤感情绪。

when people recollect the past, they still feel the deep-rooted pain, but they did not cherish at that time and everything can't come back. Life is like a dream and the past is like the smoke and the beauty can't come back. The last two sentences show the inner sadness of the poet. The painful emotion stays in his heart for a long time.

　　This poem expresses Li Shangyin's deep missing to his dead wife, thinking of the beautiful days with his wife, which can't come back. According to the verses, we also can interpret the poem as the lament for the past youth, as well as the thought and sigh for part of his own life experience. The three kinds of understanding express the emotion that once possessed but lost forever.

庄周梦蝶

　　庄周（约前369—前286）是战国时期道家学派的代表人物，一般被称为"庄子"。在他的著作《庄子》中记载了这样一个故事：庄周梦见自己变成一只蝴蝶，飘飘荡荡，十分自在，完全忘记了自己是庄周。他醒来之后感到十分疑惑，分不清是庄周做梦变成蝴蝶，还是蝴蝶做梦变成了庄周。这个故事充满了浪漫的情感和丰富的哲思，引发后世文人骚客的共鸣，成为他们经常吟咏的题目。

Zhuang Zhou Dreamt To Be A Butterfly

Zhuang Zhou (approx. 369 B.C.-286 B.C.) was the representative scholar of Taoism in the Warring States Period (475 B.C.-221 B.C.), generally called Zhuangzi. In his book *Zhuangzi*, there is such a story: Zhuang Zhou dreamt to be a butterfly flying in the air freely, and totally forgot that he was Zhuangzi himself. When he woke up, he was very confused because he didn't know whether it was Zhuang Zhou who became a butterfly or it was a butterfly that turned into Zhuang Zhou. The story is filled with romantic sentiments and profound philosophy, which struck a chord with later writers. So it became the subject they frequently cite.

- 《梦蝶图》刘贯道（元）

此图取材于"庄周梦蝶"的典故。炎夏树荫下，庄周袒胸仰卧石榻之上，一对蝴蝶翩然而乐，点明画题。

Dreaming of Butterflies, by Liu Guandao (Yuan Dynasty, 1206-1368)

It was based on the story of "Zhuang Zhou dreaming to become a butterfly", with Zhuang Zhou baring his breast and lying on a stone bed under a tree in summer, and a pair of butterflies flying happily which indicated the theme of the painting.

> 唐朝女诗人

根据史料记载，在有姓名可考的唐朝2200多位诗人当中，有200多位女诗人，她们保留下来的诗歌作

- 彩色釉陶托鹦鹉女俑（唐）
  Color-glazed Clay Statue of a Woman Holding a Parrot (Tang Dynasty, 618-907)

> Poetesses of Tang Dynasty

According to historical materials, there are 200 poetesses among the 2,200 poets already known in the Tang Dynasty. The number of the poems that are created by them and remain is 586. The situation is rare in every dynasty in China. Among these poetesses of the Tang Dynasty, the most famous are Li Ye, Xue Tao and Yu Xuanji, whose poems that remains are also the most. Among them, Li Ye is the earliest while Yu Xuanji is the latest. What's more, the Empress Wu Zetian and her most capable woman official Shangguan Wan'er also have excellent works. They are outstanding representatives of poetesses in the Tang

品总和大约是586首，这在中国古代各朝各代中实属罕见。而这些唐代女诗人中，最著名且作品现存最多的就是三大女诗人李冶、薛涛、鱼玄机。其中李冶的时代最早，鱼玄机最晚。此外，女皇帝武则天和她最得力的女官上官婉儿也有不俗的作品问世，她们同样是唐朝杰出女诗人的代表。

这几位女诗人之所以能够在诗坛占有一席之地，在于她们共同具有的一些特点：她们都敢于冲破封建社会礼教的约束，争取自己的幸福和利益，不随便屈服于命运；她们都具有自己独立的社会生活和社交圈子，而不是像大部分唐朝妇女那样，躲在闺阁里一辈子都无法接触外面的世界；她们都极具才华，有文学素养和独特个性，具备开阔的胸襟视野和敏锐的洞察力。从传奇般的人生经历中就可以看出她们的与众不同，从她们的作品中就可以读出这些女诗人在那个时代的标新立异。

Dynasty as well.

The reason why these poetesses can play a role in poetry is that they are brave to break out of the feudal ethics to pursue their own happiness and benefit, not giving in to the destiny. They all have independent life and social intercourse rather than other women, staying in their rooms without connection with the outer world. They are all talented with good education and unique character, and have open mind and keen insight. From their legendary life experience, we can see that they are different. From their works, we can know how new and unique these poetesses were at that time.

- 墓室壁画众女侍（唐）
  Tomb Fresco of Several Maids (Tang Dynasty, 618-907)

李冶

李冶（？—784），字季兰，年幼就入道教成为女道士，在少女怀春的年纪结交游览道观的文人墨客，并与他们谈论诗词，所作诗歌很多都是表达爱慕思念之情。但是碍于身份，她始终未能婚嫁，晚年因为声名远播被唐玄宗召见，却赶上"安史之乱"失踪于乱世。虽然李冶终生并未婚配，却写出了一首非常有名的作品，被评价为对夫妻关系最通透的解读。

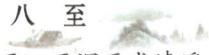

八 至

至近至远东西，至深至浅清溪。
至高至明日月，至亲至疏夫妻。

在古代封建宗法制度中，夫为妻纲，就是说妻子的生活要一切以丈夫为重心。夫妻之间的爱情是不平等的，一切遵从丈夫的要求。任何人的婚姻都由宗法制度决定，而不是以个人的情感为依据，即使双方都有爱情，能否成为夫妻也要根据封建婚姻制度来决定，这种爱情也是由封建制度维持着的。李冶用一首《八至》揭示了当时社会夫妻

Li Ye

Li Ye (?-784) whose courtesy name is Jilan, became a famale Taoist when she was young. She made friends with poets and writers and talked about poems. Most of her poems express her love and missing. However, because of her status, she couldn't marry. When she was old, she was so famous that Emperor Li Longji called in her, but she was lost in the An-Shi Rebellion (755-763). Although Li Ye didn't marry all her life, she wrote a well-known poem which is remarked to be the most appropriate description of spouses.

Eight Extreme

The nearest and farthest is the distance of east and west,
The deepest and shallowest is the depth of the clean creek.
The highest and brightest is the sun and the moon,
The closest and most distant is the distance between spouses.

In the feudal ethics, husband guides wife, which is to say, wife's life must center on husband. The love between spouses is not equal. Wife must obey all requirements of the husband. Marriage

关系的本质：表面上看起来好像亲密得"至近""至深""至高"，实际上却疏淡得"至远""至浅""至明"，如同"东"和"西"、"深"和"浅"之间的对立。"东西""清溪""日月"都是比喻，暗示丈夫和妻子之间的关系，肉体结合在一起好像彼此很亲近，其实内心因为地位的不平等及灵魂的隔阂而情浅疏远。阐释了封建社会"至亲至疏夫妻"的辩证观点。这首诗在当时那个年代和社会来看，都是非常大胆的文字。

薛涛

薛涛（约768—832），字洪度，出身歌伎，却是蜀中四大才女之一。因为她丝毫不输男子的才华，当时四川节度使曾打算请朝廷授以校书郎的官衔给她，虽然未能实现，但成为一桩美谈，她的美名"女校书"也被广为传颂。薛涛跟李冶和鱼玄机一样，终生渴望感情的归宿，然而却只能孤独终老。她晚年隐居成都浣花溪，自制一种桃红色的小彩笺用以写诗，后人称为"薛涛笺"，为时人所追捧。

is decided by the patriarchal clan system, but not personal sentiments. Even though both have love, whether they can get married depends on feudal marriage system. This kind of love is maintained by the feudal system. Li Ye uses the poem *Eight Extreme* to uncover the essence of spouse: It seems that the spouse are the closest, nearest, deepest and highest, but in fact they are the most distant, farthest, shallowest and brightest, just like east and west, deep and shallow. "East and west", "stream" and "the sun and the moon" are all analogy and suggest the relationship between husband and wife. Their bodies get together, which seems close, but actually they are far away with each other because they are not equal and there is estrangement between their souls. The poem shows the dialectical opinion that "the closest and most distant is spouses", which is very bold at that time.

Xue Tao

Xue Tao (approx.768-832) whose courtesy name is Hongdu was born as a singer but she was one of the four most talented women in Shu District. Because her talent was as good as that of men, the

四川成都望江楼公园内的薛涛像(图片提供：FOTOE)
Statue of Xue Tao in Wangjianglou Park in Chengdu City, Sichuan Province

governor of Sichuan planned to ask the royal court to appoint her as an official. Though it was not realized, it became a good story and her nice reputation "Woman Official" was spread. Xue Tao is like Li Ye and Yu Xuanji, longing for a home for sentiments all life but they could only live alone. She lived in seclusion in Huanhua Stream in Chengdu City and made a kind of pink sheet to write poems, which is called "Xue Tao Letter" and liked by people at that time.

Most of her poems express the happiness and sorrow felt by a woman and the famous poem *Spring View Verse* is the representative.

青瓷奏乐女俑（唐）
Celadon Porcelain Statue of a Woman Playing Musical Instrument (Tang Dynasty, 618-907)

她的诗歌大多表达身为女子所感受到的悲欢情愁，著名的《春望词》就是其中代表。

春望词四首

花开不同赏，花落不同悲。
欲问相思处，花开花落时。

揽草结同心，将以遗知音。
春愁正断绝，春鸟复哀吟。

风花日将老，佳期犹渺渺。
不结同心人，空结同心草。

那堪花满枝，翻作两相思。
玉箸垂朝镜，春风知不知？

这组联章诗作，通过描写春天的风景，诗人触景生情，情与景交融在一起。第一首写花开、花落，感慨人与人之间的相思之情如同花开花落一样幻生幻灭，心生相思悲情；第二首写草和春鸟，草能同心，人却知音难觅，春日生愁，连鸟的鸣叫都听起来哀伤；第三首写春风和同心草，倾诉青春飞逝，却人不同心的哀愁；第四首写花和春风，借问风可否知道人的相思之

Spring View Verse (Four Verses)
Not appreciate the blooms at the same time;
Not feel sad about the drop flowers at the same time,
To ask where I miss you,
When the flowers bloom and wither.

I pick grass to weave a node,
And give it to my lovely friend.
The spring sorrow is breaking off;
The spring bird is singing sadly again.

Beautiful flowers are getting old,
But good times are still far away.
I cannot find my Mr. Right,
Weaving the node in vain.

A tree of flowers cannot bear;
It turns into two kinds of missing.
Jade chopsticks lying in front of the morning mirror.
Spring wind, do you understand?

These four verses describe the scenery of the spring and mix the sentiments with scenery. The first poem is about the blooming and dropping of flowers. It says that the missing between people is instable just like the blooming and dropping of flowers, which

- 四川成都薛涛井

薛涛井位于四川成都望江楼公园内，旧名"玉女津"，井中水质清澈。明代蜀地官员曾汲取井水仿制薛涛笺，薛涛井因此而得名。

Xue Tao Well in Chengdu City, Sichuan Province

Xue Tao Well is located in Wangjianglou Park in Chengdu City, Sichuan Province and once called "Beauty Well". Water in the well was clear and officials of Ming Dynasty (1368-1644) in Shu District once dug up water from the well to make Xue Tao Letter. This was why the well got its name.

情。女诗人在诗中借助内心的移情作用，将情倾注于景物之中，文字看似处处是景，皆寄托诗人款款深情，表达了心中无尽之愁思。

鱼玄机

鱼玄机（约844—868），字幼薇，一字蕙兰。她是在被丈夫抛弃之后入道成为女道士的，这个身份为她获得了和文人墨客们饮酒作诗、自由往来的机会。她的住所门庭若市，跟文人们的风流韵事也广为流传。然而作为一位女性，鱼玄机根本无法掌握自己的感情命运。她终其一生，对自己的前夫和诸多文人都付出满腔真情，然而仍然

makes readers sad. The second poem is about grass and spring birds. Grass can understand each other but people cannot find their bosom friends. So the poetess was worried as well and the sound of birds is sad. The third poem is about spring winds and grass, telling people that the youth is passing quickly, but people cannot understand each other. The fourth poem is about flowers and spring wind. The poetess asked the spring winds whether it knew human sorrow in order to pour her sentiments into the scenery with the moving of her emotion. The poems seem to describe scenery everywhere. In fact the poetess based her deep love in them to express her endless sorrow.

• 《元机诗意图》改琦（清）

这幅作品是唐代女诗人鱼玄机的画像。清代的康熙皇帝名玄烨，为避讳，改称为鱼元机。

Poetic Painting of Yuanji, by Gai Qi (Qing Dynasty, 1616-1911)

This is the portrait of the poetess of the Tang Dynasty, Yu Xuanji. Emperor Kangxi's name was Xuanye and in order to avoid the taboo of his name, people called her Yu Yuanji instead.

Yu Xuanji

Yu Xuanji (appox.844-868) whose courtesy name is Huilan, or Youwei. It is after she was abandoned by her husband that she became a female Taoist. This status earns her the opportunity to get together and drink with the poets and writers. Her home was crowed, and her relationship with the poets is widely spread. However, as a woman, Yu Xuanji could not master her own sentiments and destiny. She gave out true love to her ex-husband and many writers all her life, but she remained single and at last she was sentenced to death as a result of killing her maidservant out of jealousy. No matter whether it is true, her hope for love is obvious. Her verse "It is easy to obtain invaluable treasure but it is difficult to find a man loving you" becomes the description of thousands of girls who are looking for true love.

Present To the Neighbor Girl

Shy and cover her face with the silk sleeve,
Worried about the spring and get up late to make up.
It is easy to obtain invaluable treasure,
But it is difficult to find a man with true heart.

一身，最终因妒生恨、杀婢女而被处死。不管这个罪名是否属实，她对感情的渴求都可见一斑。她的一句"易求无价宝，难得有心郎"，成为万千古代痴情女子追求真爱而不得的心情写照。

赠邻女

羞日遮罗袖，愁春懒起妆。
易求无价宝，难得有心郎。
枕上潜垂泪，花间暗断肠。
自能窥宋玉，何必恨王昌。

这是一首大胆表露女子内心渴望真情的诗。此诗是写给邻家姑娘的。前两句写这个姑娘怕见阳光故以罗袖遮掩太阳；内心忧愁早晨懒得起来梳妆。第三、第四句说明愁绪的原因：男人们薄情寡义，想要找一个真心对自己的男人，比找一件无价之宝更为困难。第五、第六句写这个姑娘因为哀愁，连睡着时也偷偷地哭泣，在花园里也无心赏花而暗自伤神。在最后两句中，鱼玄机鼓励这个弱女子争取主动，自己去寻找"有心郎"，不必为负心汉浪费自己的精力，努力追求属于自己的生活。

Weeping quietly on the pillow,
Feeling pains among the flowers.
If you could see Song Yu,
You don't need to hate Wang Chang.

This is a poem that expresses the girl's hope for loving bravely and it is for the neighbor girl. The first sentence says that the girl is shy to look at the sun so she uses her sleeve to cover the face. She is unhappy and doesn't want to get up to make up. The third and fourth sentences indicate the reason for sadness. Men are easy to forget their oath so it is more difficult to find a man loving you than find invaluable treasure. The fifth

• 《纨扇仕女图》闵贞（清）
Portrait of a Lady Holding a Fan, by Min Zhen (Qing Dynasty, 1616-1911)

这首诗在当时妇女大都不能左右自己的婚姻爱情乃至命运的现实状况下，显得尤其特立独行，因此鱼玄机在当时和后世都被社会视为异类。在诗歌成就上，鱼玄机的诗表现出过人的才华，当时许多著名文人都与她多有唱和之作，能得到这些才子们的肯定，充分说明她的诗歌水平。

and sixth sentences say that the girl is so unhappy that she weeps when asleep and feels sad when playing in the garden. In the last two sentences, Yu Xuanji encourages the girl actively to pursue a man loving her, but not waste energy for the heartless men, trying to get her own happy life.

This poem seems unique at the time when women could not master their marriage and love, even their destiny. So Yu Xuanji was seen as eccentric at that time and afterworld. Yu Xuanji manifested exceptional talent in the aspect of poem creation and many poets had cooperative poems with her. It fully indicates that the level of her poems is high with the appreciation of the talented.

宋玉与王昌

宋玉是战国时期楚国的大夫，著名的文学家，中国古代四大美男之一，才华与美貌名垂千古。王昌是魏晋时期的才子，样貌俊美，很受欢迎。

Song Yu and Wang Chang

Song Yu, a senior official (*Dafu*) of State Chu in Warring States Period (475 B.C.-221 B.C.), was a famous writer, one of the Four Most Handsome Men in ancient China whose beauty was spread widely. He was the synonym for handsome and talented man. Wang Chang was a talent in the Western Jin and Eastern Jin dynasties (265-420), who had appealing appearance and welcomed by people.

武则天

　　武则天（624—705），是中国古代一位卓越超群的女政治家，她不仅是一个敢于挑战男权统治者并成功成为女皇的人，也是一位杰出的诗人。"则天"是唐中宗给她的尊号，她后来造了一个字"曌"作为自己的名，意思是日月临空、照耀大地，由此可见其恢宏气度和勃勃野心。尽管具有超越男性的铁腕和胆识，但武则天作为女性，依然在诗作中表达出了女性多情婉约的特质，自制的商调曲《如意娘》表现出了她柔情似水的浪漫性格：

Wu Zetian

Wu Zetian (624-705) is a prominent woman politician in ancient China. She is not only the one who succeeds in challenging the man power to become

著名诗人与唐诗作品 Famous Poets and Works

• 陕西西安唐乾陵无字碑

唐乾陵是唐高宗和武则天合葬的帝陵，无字碑位于乾陵东侧，是为女皇帝武则天所立，与西侧唐高宗李治的述圣记碑相呼应。碑上未刻一字，据说来自武则天的临终遗言："己之功过，留待后人评说。"

Blank Gravestone of Tangqian Tomb in Xi'an City, Shaanxi Province

Tangqian Tomb is the royal tomb of Emperor Li Zhi and Wu Zetian. The Blank Gravestone is located at the east side of Qian Tomb and is built for Empress Wu Zetian, opposite to the Stating Sage Gravestone of Emperor Li Zhi on the west side. It has no inscription, which is said to follow the last words of Wu Zetian: "My merits and defects remain to be remarked by later generations."

• 武则天像
Portrait of Wu Zetian

如意娘

看朱成碧思纷纷，憔悴支离为忆君。
不信比来常下泪，开箱验取石榴裙。

　　这首诗主要表现女子思念情郎追忆过往的憔悴苦闷的情绪。诗意：我常常想念你，以至于错把红色看成了绿色。对你的思念让我憔悴。你若不相信我为你流下的眼泪，请打开我的衣箱，拿出我的石榴裙验证一下，那上面还有我的斑斑泪痕。

● 仕女俑（唐）
Status of Maid (Tang Dynasty, 618-907)

an empress but also a brilliant poetess. "Zetian" is a name given by Emperor Li Xian and she created a character *Zhao* as her name. It means the sun and the moon are in the sky to illuminate the earth, from which we can see her broad bearing and ambition. Though she is even more brave and strict than men, she still expresses the character of affection and grace as a woman. The song *Ruyi Lady* created by herself indicates the romantic character of her tender passion.

Ruyi Lady

Touched by red flowers turning into green,
Languished and sad while missing you.
If not believe I weep out of missing,
Please open my case to see the stains on the red dress.

　　This poem mainly expresses the emotion of women who miss their lovers and the past days. I often miss you so that I take red as green. The missing of you makes me languished. If you do not believe my tears for you, please open my case and look at my pink dress, for there are tear stains on it.

上官婉儿

上官婉儿（664—710），是武则天当政时的得力助手，同时也是初唐著名诗人、大臣上官仪的孙女。她继承家学，诗文创作都属一流，并且帮助武则天进用文人学士，自身文学造诣极高。

彩书怨

叶下洞庭初，思君万里余。
露浓香被冷，月落锦屏虚。
欲奏江南曲，贪封蓟北书。
书中无别意，惟怅久离居。

诗意：秋天到了，洞庭湖边的秋叶纷纷落下，我想念在万里之外蓟北的你。露水很浓，睡觉的被子抵挡不住深秋的寒意，我因思念你而彻夜难眠。月亮落下去了，色彩斑斓的屏风因为没有月光的照耀而看不见了。我热切地想弹奏一首江南曲，给蓟北的你写一封书信。信中没有别的意思，只惆怅你我二人长久两地分居。

这首诗主要描写一个女子怀念她离居已久的丈夫。前两句就暗示这个与丈夫"久离居"的女子独守

Shangguan Wan'er

Shangguan Wan'er (664-710) was the right-hand man of Empress Wu Zetian then, and was a granddaughter of Shangguan Yi who was a famous poet and official of the early Tang Dynasty. She inherited the learning handed down in her family and her poems were excellent. She also helped Wu Zetian select literates and scholars, so the level of her literature was high.

Colorful Letter of Complaint

Leaves just drop into the Dongting Lake,
I miss you thousands of miles away.
Much dew so I feel cold in the fragrant quilt,
The moon sets down and the screen is unclear.
I want to play a song from the south of Yangtze River,
But greedy to write letters to you in north Jibei.
Nothing special written in the letters,
Only sadness for us living separately.

General idea: It is autumn and leaves beside Dongting Lake all drop. I miss you thousands of miles away in Jibei. There is much dew and the quilt is not enough to keep out the coldness. I cannot fall asleep all night because I miss you much. The moon sets down and the screen is

空房的孤寂之感。后两句说明写信的目的，没有时间写别的，只是为了向丈夫表达和他离居已久的惆怅心情。

上官婉儿的诗作和其他女诗人一样，都侧重表达女性内心思想感情的变化和真实感受，从自身角度出发描写女性的内心世界。

hard to see without moonlight. I want to play a song from the south of the Yangtze River but I choose to write a letter to you in Jibei. There are no other things in the letter but only my sadness for us living separately in two places for long.

The poem mainly describes a woman who is missing her husband away from home for a long time. The first two sentences suggest that the woman feels lonely for living separately with her husband. The last two sentences indicate the purpose of writing the letter. There is no time for other things but just her sadness for living apart from each other.

Poems written by Shangguan Wan'er are the same with those of other poetesses, which focus on expressing the variation of inner thoughts and sentiments of women and their real feelings. They describe women's inner world from their own aspects.

- 《洞庭东山图》赵孟頫（元）
East Mountain of Dongting, by Zhao Mengfu (Yuan Dynasty, 1206-1368)

> 脍炙人口的唐诗　　　> Celebrated Tang Poetries

咏　鹅

骆宾王

鹅鹅鹅，曲项向天歌。
白毛浮绿水，红掌拨清波。

Goose

Luo Binwang

Goose, Goose, Goose!
With a long-crooked neck sing to the sky.
White feathers floating on green water,
With red-webbed feet stirring in blue wave.

咏鹅

《咏鹅》是与王勃、杨炯、卢照邻齐名的"初唐四杰"之一的骆宾王7岁时写的诗，从一个儿童的视角描写鹅在水中嬉戏的神态，文笔生动活泼。

首句连用三个鹅字，模仿鹅的声音，接着描写鹅正仰着脖子向着天高声歌唱的姿态。白色的鹅毛轻轻地浮在水面上，红色的鹅掌在划

Goose

The poem *Goose* was written by Luo Binwang, one of the Four Distinguished of Early Tang Dynasty at the age of seven. It describes the geese playing in the water in the eye of a child with a vivid and vigorous style of writing.

The poem begins with three "goose" which sounds like the goose in Chinese, and then makes a picture of several geese singing with upturned necks. The geese swim with white plumage tenderly

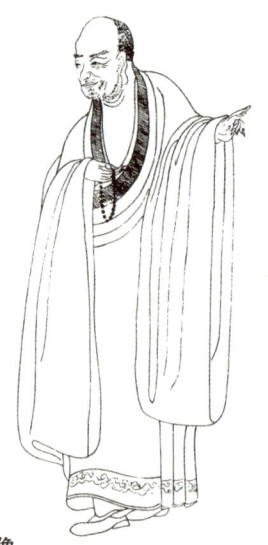

• 骆宾王像
Portrait of Luo Binwang

floating on the water and red webs paddling forward and triggering layers of waves. It's vividly sketched out that the geese are swimming in the water with naive appearance. White plumage and red webs make a good contrast in color, constitutes a beautiful picture of "geese swimming", and shows the bright and cheerful mood when children are watching geese.

Luo Binwang was a gifted child then. Under the influence of his grandfather, he was able to read and write when he was very young. The poem *Goose* became widespread once it had come out, and became popular which was studied and recited by most children at that time. Because of this, Luo Binwang was named "Child Prodigy of Jiangnan (the area of south of the Yangtze River)".

Luo Binwang was equally famous as Wang Bo, Yang Jiong and Lu Zhaolin for his literary achievement, and these four men were called "Four Distinguished of Early Tang Dynasty". He gained reputation nationwide due to the article *Official Call to Arms for Li Jingye* (calling for crusade against the rein of government by Wu Zetian in behalf of Li Jingye, a minister in Tang Dynasty). Even the current ruler, Wu Zetian, the

水前行，拨弄出一层层的水纹。鹅在水中游来游去、憨态可掬的模样被生动地勾勒出来，白毛和红掌互相映衬，构成一幅美丽的"白鹅嬉水图"，表现出小朋友明亮欢快的心情。

骆宾王儿时天资聪颖，受祖父影响启蒙较早，很早就能习文写诗，《咏鹅》一诗广为流传，成为孩童们争相学习背诵的流行唐诗，因此骆宾王被称为"江南神童"。

骆宾王与王勃、杨炯、卢照邻齐名，被称为"初唐四杰"。一篇《代李敬业传檄天下文》令他一举成名天下知。连文章的讨伐对象武则天本人都在读过其文之后极为震动，夸奖此文，并且责问宰相为何没有早点发现和重用骆宾王这个人才。

person he criticized in the article, was deeply impressed by his writing. She gave praise to the article and called the prime minister (in feudal China) to account for his ignorance of such an elite.

骆宾王与《代李敬业传檄天下文》

骆宾王不仅以诗歌见长，文章也雄伟峭劲，《代李敬业传檄天下文》就是他的代表作。唐光宅元年（684），身为太后的武则天废去刚登基的中宗李显，另立李旦为帝，自己临朝称制，想进一步登位称帝。这引起一些忠于唐室的大臣的愤怒。身为开国元勋李勣之孙的李敬业，以已故太子李贤为号召，在扬州起兵，反抗武氏。骆宾王被李敬业罗致入幕府，军中的书檄均出自他的手笔。这篇檄文立论严正，先声夺人，列数武则天的罪状，借此号召天下共同起兵，起到了很大的宣传鼓动作用。据《新唐书》所载，武则天初观此文时还嬉笑自若，当读到"一抔之土未干，六尺之孤安在"一句时，惊问是谁写的，叹道："有如此才，而使之沦落不偶，宰相之过也！"

Luo Binwang and His *Official Call to Arms for Li Jingye*

Luo Binwang was not only outstanding in poetry, but also a great writer with majestic style of writing, and the *Official Call to Arms for Li Jingye* was his master work. At the first year of Guangzhai (Tang Dynasty, 684), Wu Zetian, the mother of the emperor (Taihou) deprived Li Xian the new emperor of his status, and supported Li Dan to be the emperor. She interfered in national affairs, established the regime with the ambition of being the emperor herself. All these infuriated ministers in the imperial court who was loyal to the Tang Dynasty. Being the grandson of Li Ji (who was the founding general of the Tang Dynasty), Li Jingye, in the name of the deceased prince Li Xian, started the revolt in Yangzhou to fight against Wu's rein. Luo Binwang was employed by Li Jingye, and wrote all the official call to arms. Luo made a strict and firm argument in this article, spread out a list of charges of Wu Zetian to make a striking beginning, and used all these to call for the fight against Wu. It turned out to play a role of propaganda and agitation. According to *New Book of Tang Dynasty*, Wu Zetian didn't take it seriously when she first read it. However, when she came to the sentence "The soil on the tomb of the late emperor is still wet (the late emperor has just passed away), but our new young emperor has been sent to exile to a place nobody knows", she was astonished and asked who the author was. She said, "It's the Prime Minister's fault to let the person with such talent turn to be a rebel."

送杜少府之任蜀州

王勃

城阙辅三秦，风烟望五津。
与君离别意，同是宦游人。
海内存知己，天涯若比邻。
无为在歧路，儿女共沾巾。

Seeing Magistrate Du off to *Shu*

Wang Bo

Capital Chang'an was surrounded by the three Qin,
In the mist I looked at the five ports.
We both are wanderers post-seeking,
So we share the same sad feeling of parting.
If we have bosom friends in this world,
It can draw the distant place closer like a neighbor.
Don't separate at the cross road,
To shed tears when parting from each other.

送杜少府之任蜀州

王勃（650—676）出身望族，天资聪颖，被视为"神童"，17岁就显露才华，与杨炯、卢照邻、骆宾王齐名为"初唐四杰"，名气居四杰之首。他成年之后因写出千古名篇散文《滕王阁序》名声大噪，滕王阁也因此得名。然而，王勃才华早露，人生两起两落，后在旅行途中发生意外溺水而早亡，实为诗坛一件憾事。

《送杜少府之任蜀州》是一首相当有名的送别诗，也是王勃诗歌的代表作品。"海内存知己，天涯若比邻"是中国人表达友谊的经典佳句，也是经常在送别时使用的离

Seeing Magistrate Du off to Shu

Wang Bo (650-676), was born in a noble family. He was so gifted to be called "Child Prodigy" who had shown talent at the age of 17. He, together with Yang Jiong, Lu Zhaolin and Luo Binwang, were called "Four Distinguished of Early Tang Dynasty", but Wang Bo ranked the first among the four. It was the famous-through-ages article *Preface of Pavilion of Prince Teng* which was written when he was young that brought so much fame to him as well as the Pavilion of Prince Teng. So young as Wang Bo was when he became famous, he went through two ups and downs in his life. Wang Bo was drowned by accident in his journey at a very young age. His death was a great

● 王勃像
Portrait of Wang Bo

pity for Chinese poetry.

Seeing Magistrate Du off to Shu was a famous farewell poem as well as Wang Bo's master work. "If we have bosom friends in this world, it can draw the distant place closer like a neighbor" became a classic quote when the Chinese express their friendship, frequently used as blessing words when seeing friends off. The general meaning of this poem is: Chang'an, the farewell place was surrounded by what was called Sanqin in ancient times. The five harbors in Ba-Shu seemed to be able seen with wind and smoke filling the air. Ba-Shu (present Sichuan) was the destination the friend headed for. We are all people who secure an official position far away from home, and it's hard to expect the next time when we reunite. However, no matter where you are, as long as we are confidants, we will never be separated by distance. Therefore, please don't be sad like a sentimental girl, letting tears wet the clothes.

别祝语。全诗的大概意思是：古代称为三秦的地方环绕着长安城，这里是指送别的地方长安。风烟弥漫似乎能望见巴蜀的五大渡口，这是指明友人要去的地方是巴蜀（今四川）。我们都是远离故乡，出外做官之人，此次一别又不知何时能再见。不管你在哪里，只要是知己，即使相隔再远，都好像还在一起。所以不要在离别时哀愁忧伤，像多愁善感的女孩一样，任泪水打湿衣裳。

登鹳雀楼

王之涣

白日依山尽，黄河入海流。
欲穷千里目，更上一层楼。

Ascending the Stork Tower

Wang Zhihuan
The sunset glow is fading away behind the mountain,
The Yellow River is running towards the sea.
If you want to enjoy a grander sight,
Shall go up to a higher step.

登鹳雀楼

在浪漫主义诗人王之涣（688—742）之前，唐朝的亭台楼阁数不胜数，遍布各地。其中有一座鹳雀楼却因为王之涣的一首诗《登鹳雀楼》而名扬天下。后世许多文人墨客都因此诗慕名而来，如今鹳雀楼已经消失在历史的尘埃之中，只有从王之涣这首20字的诗中想象它的风采。全诗的大概意思是：夕阳依傍着西山慢慢地消失在天的尽头，滚滚的黄河水汹涌奔流进入东海。如果想把这广阔无垠的秀丽风光全都观赏到，那就要再上一层城楼才能登高望远。这首诗文笔流畅，如行云流水一般，将登楼赏景的过程简洁完整地描述出来，让人联想到一幅动态的风景图画。慢慢落下的夕阳映衬着流向东边的黄河水，读

Ascending the Stork Tower

In the era of the life of Wang Zhihuan (688-742), a romanticist poet, there were thousands of pavilions throughout China. Among all those pavilions, Stork Tower (Yongji, Shanxi Province) became outstanding across the country because of Wang Zhihuan's poem, *Ascending the Stork Tower*, attracting generations of poets and writers to visit. However, the Stork Tower has disappeared in the dust of history now, only leaving us imagining its beauty according to the 20-character verse. The main idea of this poem is: The sunset is disappearing slowly at the end of the sky with mountains in the background. The turbulent Yellow River is roaring and surging towards the east sea. If you want to enjoy all the vast and majestic scenery, you need to step up higher. This poem shows a natural and flowing style of writing, like floating

者跟着诗中的视角登上楼台，楼外风景尽收眼底。

诗人的思绪不是停留在眼前自然的风景，而进入想象的空间，视野穿越时空，扩展到更深远的意境。"欲穷千里目，更上一层楼"已经不只是指登楼，而是如同经历人生一样，只有拥有更加广阔的胸怀、更加高远的视野，才能海纳百川，广视万物，看到别人所看不到的本质，观察到更加深刻的内涵，才会有更深邃的思想和更远大的抱负，创造更优秀的成就。所谓"登

clouds and flowing water. It makes a complete description of the process of climbing and sightseeing but also in a concise style, and guides readers to see a dynamic landscape picture: The sunset slowing disappearing with the Yellow River flowing eastward. Following the visual perspective of the poet, readers also step on the tower, and enjoy a whole view of the scenery outside the tower.

The thoughts of the poet not only stopped at the natural landscape before his eyes, but also went further into the space of imagination, traveled through time and space, and extended to more profound artistic conception. "You can enjoy a grander sight, by climbing to a greater height", means not only climbing up the tower, but also like one's lifetime. Only by having broader mind and vaster view, can we be more tolerant, have all things in eyes, and see what others cannot see-

• 《江阁远眺图》王谔（明）
Overlook on River Attic, by Wang E (Ming Dynasty, 1368-1644)

● 山西永济鹳雀楼（图片提供：全景正片）
Stork Tower in Yongji City, Shanxi Province

高才能望远"的道理在这里得到最诗意的诠释，从而也提升了此诗的艺术品位。

the essence of the world. And we can observe more profound implication of things and have more thoughtful ideas and greater ambitions, so that we can achieve more success. It gives the most poetic explanation to the principal that "Only by climbing higher can we see further", which in turn upgrades the taste of the poem.

> 回乡偶书
>
> 贺知章
>
> 少小离家老大回，乡音无改鬓毛衰。
> 儿童相见不相识，笑问客从何处来。

> **Inspiration of Returning Home**
>
> *He Zhizhang*
> Left as a boy and back a senior to my hometown.
> Hair has turned gray but accent keeps the same.
> Kids looking at me as a total stranger,
> Ask in smile where the guest comes from?

回乡偶书

贺知章（659—约744）在朝为官，与李白是忘年之交，也是他将李白推荐给唐玄宗。他性格狂放豁达，喜欢谈笑，晚年放荡不羁，自称"四明狂客"，因为诗歌风格豪放旷达，又被称为"诗狂"。《回乡偶书》是贺知章告老还乡、一时感慨所作。诗中既有自己年纪老迈、离家太久而反被当成客人的慨叹之情，又充满了久别之后重回故里的亲切感，虽为晚年之作，却富于生活情趣。中国人讲究"落叶归根"，有多少流浪在外的游子在晚年重回故里，不想客死异乡，即使不能回来，也希望"魂归故里"。一篇《回乡偶书》将这种感情倾诉得淋漓尽致。

Inspiration of Returning Home

He Zhizhang (659-appox.744) was an official in the imperial court. He was Li Bai's good friend despite a great gap in age, and he was the person who recommended Li Bai to the emperor Tang Xuanzong. He Zhizhang was a person open and clear who likes laughing. He was unconventional and uninhibited at the old age, and called himself "Siming Madman". Because of his bold style of poetry, he was also called "Poetry Madman". *Inspiration of Returning Home* was inspired by momentary emotion when he returned home after his retire and was inspired. In this poem, the poet expressed the mixed emotion of turning into a guest after many years away from home as so aged and the intimacy he fell when returning. Although it was

全诗的大概意思：我在年少时离开家乡，到了晚年才回来。虽然我的口音并没有改变，但头发却

•《骑驴归思图》唐寅（明）
Returning Home on the Donkey, by Tang Yin (Ming Dynasty, 1368-1644)

written when he was old, it's a poem full of interests in life. The Chinese believe in "fallen leaves return to the roots", and that's why many people would return home after years of wandering life who don't want to die in strange land. Even though they are not able to return, they still wish their soul could come back. Such emotion is completely expressed in this poem.

The general idea of this poem is: I left home when I was young and returned home at the old age. Though I still keep my accent, my hair has turned gray. Nobody recognized me when children in my hometown saw me. They smiled and asked me: "My guest, where are you from?"

The first two lines of the poem are just narrative sentences, but there's an interesting turning point in the last two lines. Despite the sadness of being old and homesick, the children's naive question makes readers cannot help smiling. Every word in the poem is from natural and sincere emotion, and the language is simple unvarnished

已经斑白。家乡的孩童们看见我，没有一个认识我的，他们笑着问："客人，你是从哪里来的呀？"

全诗第一、第二句平平而叙，第三、第四句却峰回路转，别有情趣，虽然久客伤老之情令人伤感不已，但儿童笑问的场景也令人忍俊不禁。全诗感情自然真诚，语言朴实无华，不事雕琢，给人一种山河依旧、人事不同、人生易老、世事沧桑的感慨，读来余味悠长。

but clean, making readers to think more about the regular pattern that "Things are the same, but we are no more". "Life is short; things are changing" is the idea that leads us to endless thinking.

逢雪宿芙蓉山主人

刘长卿

日暮苍山远，天寒白屋贫。
柴门闻犬吠，风雪夜归人。

Guesting in Furong Mountain Cottage in Snow

Liu Changqing

The sun has gone down and mountains are far away;
Cold weather and white snow make houses poorer.
Inside the door of the yard there's dog barking;
Near the house a man is back on such windy and snowy night.

逢雪宿芙蓉山主人

刘长卿擅长五言诗，他的五言排律在名家辈出、成就斐然的盛唐时期别有特色，在诗坛占有一席之

Guesting in Furong Mountain Cottage in Snow

Liu Changqing was skilled at five-character poetry. He held his place among generations of successful masters in the prosperous period of the Tang Dynasty. Although Liu Changqing wasn't a productive poet, his works are fluent in language, and *Guesting in Furong Mountain Cottage in Snow* is just one master piece of five-character poem. The

- 《逢雪宿芙蓉山主人》诗意图
Poetic Painting of *Guesting in Furong Mountain Cottage in Snow*

青瓷狗圈（东晋）
Celadon Porcelain Dog House (Eastern Jin Dynasty, 317-420)

地。他创作的五言绝句虽然数量不多，但语言流畅，脍炙人口的名篇《逢雪宿芙蓉山主人》就是五绝中的精品。这首诗描绘的是一幅诗人在风雪之夜投宿山中贫困人家，恰逢主人归家的风雪寒山夜宿图。诗中描述：夜色降临，山路遥远，天气寒冷，山中的茅草屋在大雪中显得很单薄。诗人借宿在这里，忽然听到柴门外传来了狗叫的声音，大概是芙蓉山主人披风戴雪归来了吧。

　　这首诗四个分句，每一个分句都可以是一幅图画。第一幅画：夜色的笼罩下，远处深山苍茫，遥远曲折的山路从近处延伸到山中。第二幅画：风卷入雪弥漫空中，一个孤零零的小草屋屋顶覆盖着厚厚的积雪，镶嵌在山中显得弱小单薄。第三幅画：草屋外的狗在风雪中叫唤，仿佛看到了熟人一般。第四幅画：草屋的主人冒着呼啸的风雪在

poem depicts such a picture: The poet sought a temporary lodging in a poor village on a windy and snowy night, and met the host who was just coming back at night. It's described in the poem that when the night fell, the road ahead seemed to be even longer. It's so cold that the cottages in the mountain were frailer. The poet asked a lodging here and heard the dog's barking suddenly from the door of the garden. It's probably that the host of the Furong Mountain is back in snow.

　　Every line of this poem makes a picture. In the first picture, there's falling darkness and great mountains in distance, with a winding hill road meandering to the distant place. In the second one, the wind and snow was full of the air; a lonely cottage was covered by thick snow which seemed to be smaller and weaker as it was embedded in the mountain. The third picture is about a dog barking outside the cottage as if it was welcoming its friend. In the last picture, the host of

夜里回到家中。后两幅画虽然是诗人用语言从侧面描写，只是捕捉了狗叫的声音和他依据常理的推测，却更加突出了图画的效果，给读者留下了广阔的想象空间。后人甚至分析这位主人和诗人之间的关系，到底引起狗叫的是草屋的主人，还是诗人自己从外面进门呢？这个问题的答案恐怕要留给读过这首诗的人们自己去寻找了。

the cottage is coming back against the wind and snow. Although the last two pictures are painted indirectly with only dog's barking and the poet's guess, the description makes the situation more vivid and leave readers vast space for imagination. Readers in later generation even think of more about the relative position of the poet and the host. Was it the host or the poet himself that made the dog bark? The answer is left for us readers to explore.

江 雪

柳宗元

千山鸟飞绝，万径人踪灭。
孤舟蓑笠翁，独钓寒江雪。

River Snow

Liu Zongyuan

A hundred mountains and with no bird,
Ten thousand paths without a footprint.
A little boat, a bamboo cloak,
An old man fishing in the cold river snow.

江雪

柳宗元（773—819）是中唐时期著名的文学家、思想家。他的诗歌在简淡的格调中表现极其沉厚的感情，富有哲理和韵味，呈现出一种独特的面貌。他的代表作五言绝

River Snow

Liu Zongyuan (773-819) is a writer and thinker in the middle period of the Tang Dynasty. His poems usually express profound emotion with a style of simplicity. Full of philosophy and artistic aroma, Liu Zongyuan's poems

• 柳宗元像
Portrait of Liu Zongyuan

• 《寒江独钓图》沈周（明）

此图绘冬日风景，溪树山石，一渔翁泊舟独钓。风欲止，水无痕，景致宁静萧然，钓者斗笠蓑衣，悠然自得，正合柳宗元《江雪》诗意。

Fishing Alone on a Cold River, by Shen Zhou (Ming Dynasty, 1368-1644)

It's a painting of winter scenery, with stream, trees, mountains and stones, as well as an old fisherman fishing alone on a boat. The wind is still and the surface of water is smooth, which show a peaceful and bleak feeling. The fisherman is covered by a straw rain cape and a bamboo hat, with a poised look on his face, which is just in accordance with the meaning and atmosphere of Liu's poem.

show a unique picture. His master work, the *River Snow* manifests a far-reaching content, ranking one of the best quatrains among Tang poetry.

This poem appears to be a landscape poem, but it says more about the poet's aspiration by depicting the scenery. Above the cold river, there's freezing air and falling snow. It's all quiet around with no passengers and no flying birds. But there's still an old man wearing a straw rain cape and a leaf hat who was sitting in a lonely boat, fishing silently and suffering from cold. What hides behind the picture of such a landscape picture is the poet's own feelings and aspiration. The *River Snow* was written after he was persecuted and demoted

句《江雪》意境幽远，内涵深邃，在唐诗绝句中属于上乘之作。

《江雪》表面看似是一首山水诗，其实以景言志。冰天雪飘的寒冷江面上，周围没有行人，甚至飞鸟，万籁俱寂。只有一位披着蓑衣戴着斗笠的老翁独自驾着孤舟停留在江面上，一个人忍受寒冷和孤独默默地垂钓，这分明是一幅山水画面，而画中所暗示的却是柳宗元内心的感受和志向。《江雪》是他遭受迫害被贬永州后所作，这幅渔翁寒江独钓图是想强调他所处政治环境的恶劣，而即使孤独清冷，他也依然顽强不屈、毫无畏惧，像渔夫一样面对寒冷的风雪不为所动。诗人用极其洗练的文笔，勾勒出一幅渔翁在白雪茫茫的寒江上独钓的画面，表现的是他的坚强意志和不同流合污的高贵品质。诗歌看似平凡，其实内涵深刻，暗含志向，是一首励志名诗。

to Yongzhou. The picture in the poem indicates the harsh political situation he faced. However, no matter how lonely and helpless, the poet was still resolute and fearless, just as the fisherman who remained unmoved in the face of cold wind and snow. Liu used the most succinct language, sketched out the picture of a lonely fisherman on a river covered by snow, and expressed his noble qualities of persistency and integrity. It's a short poem which looks ordinary, but in fact, it's an inspirational poem which is profound with implications.

- 《秋江渔隐图》马远（宋）
  Fishing on Autumn River, by Ma Yuan (Song Dynasty, 960-1279)

枫桥夜泊

张继

月落乌啼霜满天，
江枫渔火对愁眠。
姑苏城外寒山寺，
夜半钟声到客船。

Mooring by Maple Bridge at Night

Zhang Ji

At moonset cry the crows, striking the frosty sky,
Dimly shone fishing boats' light beneath maples sadly lie.
Beyond the city wall, is Temple of Cold Hill,
Bells break the ship-borne roamer's dream and midnight still.

枫桥夜泊

《枫桥夜泊》是盛唐时期的诗人张继在旅途中途经寒山寺时所作。自从张继的《枫桥夜泊》问世

Mooring by Maple Bridge at Night

Mooring by Maple Bridge at Night was written by poet Zhang Ji of the prosperous period of the Tang Dynasty. He wrote this poem when passing by *Hanshan* Temple (Temple of Cold Hill) during his journey. Ever since this poem came out, the Temple of Cold Hill has gained a national reputation and become a famous place of interest.

● 苏州寒山寺

寒山寺位于江苏省苏州城外的枫桥镇，建于梁代天监年间，距今已有1500多年。寺中这座六角形重檐亭阁，就是以"夜半钟声到客船"而闻名遐迩的钟楼。

Hanshan Temple (Temple of Cold Hill) in Suzhou City

Hanshan Temple (Temple of Cold Hill) is located in Maple Bridge Town, outside Suzhou City, Jiangsu Province. It was built during the Period Tianjian (502-519), in Liang Dynasty which was 1,500 years from now. The hexagonal multi-eave attic in the temple is the famous bell tower in the verse "Bells break the ship-borne roamer's dream and midnight still."

后，寒山寺因此名扬天下，成为著名的游览胜地。

全诗大概意思：月亮已落，乌鸦在附近啼叫，天气寒冷已经结霜了，江上枫桥边闪着星星点点的渔火，只剩我独自忧愁无法入睡，心中寂寞。苏州城外那寒山古寺里，半夜敲响的钟声传到了我乘坐的客船里。寂静的秋夜，远处传来的钟声、星点的渔火和停泊的客船，勾勒出一幅清幽明净的图画。这首诗有声有色，有情有景，情景交融，表达出诗人在旅途中孤寂忧愁的情绪，实属千古名篇。

The general meaning of this poem is: The moon has gone down when crows are crying around. In the cold and frosting dawn, there are dimly glimmering lights from the fishing boats beside the Maple Bridge on the river. Everyone has fallen asleep, but I am still awake, lonely and gloomy. In the boat I take, I can hear the ringing bell at the night, which is from the *Hanshan* Temple (Temple of Cold Hill), outside the city of Gusu. The tranquil autumn night, the bell from distance, scattered lights and the boat moored at the port comprise a picture peaceful and clear. This poem contains both colors and voices, both landscape and emotion. With the feeling and setting properly blended, this poem expresses the loneliness and sadness of the poet in the journey. No wonder it's a masterpiece throughout times.

- **寒山寺外的枫桥**

枫桥位于苏州北的枫桥镇，横跨于运河支流之上。它始建于唐代，本是一座江南普通的月牙形单孔石拱桥，却因张继的《枫桥夜泊》而千古留名。

Maple Bridge outside *Hanshan* Temple (Temple of Cold Hill)

The Maple Bridge is located in Maple Bridge Town, in the north of Suzhou City, crossing above the branch of the Grand Canal. It was built in the Tang Dynasty as an ordinary single-hole stone arch bridge with crescent shape in the regions south of the Yangtze River, but became famous in history because of Zhang Ji's poem *Mooring by Maple Bridge at Night*.

游子吟

孟郊

慈母手中线，游子身上衣。
临行密密缝，意恐迟迟归。
谁言寸草心，报得三春晖！

A Song of the Travelling Son

Meng Jiao

A thread in mother's loving hand,
Makes up the clothes for her travelling son.
Knitting all her love into every stitch,
She's worrying he'd be away for too long.
How could the grateful humble grass,
Ever repay the kindness of the generous sun?

游子吟

孟郊（751—814）是中唐时期有名的诗人，人称"诗囚"，又称"诗奴"。他一生贫困潦倒，很少与外界往来，只喜欢自己在家作诗苦吟，在诗歌的字句上狠下功夫。孟郊写诗，几乎每个字都要先仔细琢磨，用时都要有根有据，并且喜欢模仿前朝，善用古体诗来创作。他因此和韩愈被后人称为"韩孟诗派"的代表，又和贾岛一起被后人称为苦吟诗人的代表。

孟郊的诗歌内容多是底层文人的穷愁困苦的怨怼情绪，除了这些主要作品，孟郊还有一些描写平凡人伦的诗作也脍炙人口、家喻户晓，比如这首有名的《游子吟》，写的是感人至深的母子之爱。一位母亲手里拿着针线，为即将远行

A Song of the Travelling Son

Meng Jiao (751-814) was a poet in the middle period of the Tang Dynasty, who was called the "Prisoner of Poetry" and the "Slave of Poetry". He suffered from difficulty and poverty all his life and seldom got connected with the outside world. His only hobby was reading and writing poems alone at home, devoting himself to pondering every word and sentence of his poems. Meng Jiao had a good thought of almost every character before writing to make sure they were from classic allusions. He also liked to imitate the writing style of the former dynasty, and was skilled at writing poems in ancient style. Therefore, he and Han Yu were regarded as the representatives of the "Han-Meng School", and he was also a representative of the poets of industrious poetry school, together with Jia Dao.

的儿子缝制衣服,一针一线都缝得仔细密实,只担心儿子不能早点归来。对于这春天阳光般深情的母爱,即便孩子有报答的心,也只如那细小的花草,怎能报答得了呢?

孝是中国传统道德的核心,中国人几千年来都倡导孝顺长辈为第一重要的事情,这首《游子吟》讲述母慈子孝的深情厚谊,得到人们的喜爱,尤其代表了天下游子对母亲的怀念感激之情,因而传诵千年,经久不衰,引起万千游子的共鸣。

● 粉彩母子如意图花口盘(清)
Pastel porcelain plate with flower-shaped rim and a Ruyi pattern of mother and son (Qing Dynasty, 1616-1911)

Most of the poems of Meng Jiao are about the difficult life and the sadness of the writers and poets in the lowest social class. Apart from these major works, Meng Jiao also wrote poems describing normal people's relationship and emotion which enjoy great popularity, and *A Song of the Travelling Son* is just one example. This poem is about the deepest and most touching love between mother and son. A mother is making a new piece of clothes with a needle and threads holding in hands. Every stitch is made carefully and firmly, containing her worry about her son's not coming back early. While the deep maternal love is like the sunshine in spring, the child is just like the little flower, receiving warmness from the sun. In face of such love, how could a child has enough to pay back?

Filial piety is the core of the Chinese culture, which is advocated as the most important thing by the Chinese for thousands of years. The poem *A Song of the Travelling Son* is about the deep love between a kindly mother and a good son, which is why it has been widely spread throughout times and never faded. It triggers the resonance of many travelling people.